BEACON STREET GIRLS

This book belongs to:

VERITAS AMICITIA GAUDIUM
truth friendship fun!

™

Who's Who

BSG

Katani Summers
a.k.a. Kgirl ... Katani has a strong fashion sense and business savvy. She is stylish, loyal & cool.

Avery Madden
Avery is passionate about all sports and animal rights. She is energetic, optimistic & outspoken.

Charlotte Ramsey
A self-acknowledged "klutz" and an aspiring writer, Charlotte is all too familiar with being the new kid in town. She is intelligent, worldly & curious.

Isabel Martinez
Her ambition is to be an artist. She was the last to join the Beacon Street Girls. She is artistic, sensitive & kind.

Maeve Kaplan-Taylor
Maeve wants to be a movie star. Bubbly and upbeat, she wears her heart on her sleeve. She is entertaining, friendly & fun.

Ms. Razzberry Pink
The stylishly pink proprietor of the "Think Pink" boutique is chic, gracious & charming.

Marty
The adopted best dog friend of the Beacon Street Girls is feisty, cuddly & suave.

Happy Lucky Thingy and alter ego Mad Nasty Thingy
Marty's favorite chew toy, it is known to reveal its alter ego when shaken too roughly. He is most often happy.

more on beaconstreetgirls.com

BEACON STREET GIRLS

Be sure to read all of our books:

SCHOLASTIC INC.

New York Toronto London Auckland Sydney
Mexico City New Delhi Hong Kong Buenos Aires

ISBN-13: 978-0-545-11165-2
ISBN-10: 0-545-11165-X

12 11 10 9 8 7 6 5 4 3 2 1   8 9 10 11 12 13/0

Printed in the U.S.A.   40

First Scholastic printing, November 2008

Series Editor: Roberta MacPhee
Art Direction: Pamela M. Esty
Book Design: Dina Barsky
Illustration: Pamela M. Esty

Friendship ... it's such a leap of faith.

CR

PART ONE

BAD NEWS

CR

CHAPTER 1

Charlotte

WISHES AND JINXES

Sunday night, way too late

I know I should be in bed already but I can't seem to fall asleep. Dad came into my room a few minutes ago and found me out on the balcony, searching the sky for the Seven Sisters—seven stars that travel together around the skies. It's the constellation that always makes me think of Mom because it was her favorite. Dad's been working like crazy on his new book and he seemed kind of distracted, but he wanted to kiss me good-night and catch up on how things are going. Dad and I have always been close—we have so many inside jokes. Like one of us will say, "Well ... there's good news and bad news. Which do you want to hear first?" And we always answer together, right at the same time, "Give me the bad news first!" I don't know why, but that always cracks us both up.

When Dad asked me what was coming up for this week, I had a whole list. It's hard to believe that just a few weeks ago, I was brand new here and worried that I was going to have to suffer through seventh grade in a new city without a single friend. When I think back on everything that's happened—meeting Maeve,

Avery, and Katani ... all the stuff that we went through before the four of us became such good friends—I feel like the luckiest girl on earth. I'm still not sure what kind of magic turned us from worst enemies into best friends. But it happened, and tonight I feel like Maeve, Katani, Avery, and I are part of a new constellation. Like four stars traveling around together!

I know I'm getting too big to wish on stars. But, it's something I started doing with Mom when I was really young. We'd sit outside together until we could see the first star come out. Then we'd trade wishes. She always said the same thing: My wish is for your wish to come true.

That seems like such a long time ago. I was only four when she died. But even though I'm almost 13 now, wishes still matter. And I ... finally feel at home. That's why, when I saw the first star tonight, I made a wish. Know what it was?

Let this last. Don't let anything change how perfect things are right now.

❦

Later, thinking back on it, Charlotte decided that all of the trouble had started with her journal entry. *It's as if I knew somehow,* she thought. *It was a jinx. I must have sensed it was all too good to be true.*

But Monday morning, sprinting down Corey Hill through the changing New England leaves, the only problem on Charlotte's mind was how to make it to school without being late. Big changes of any kind seemed a million miles away.

"Charlotte! Wait up!" Maeve Kaplan-Taylor called, her long red hair streaming behind her as she hurried to catch up with Charlotte at the corner of Summit Avenue and Beacon Street.

"Hi, Maeve!" Charlotte slowed her pace down by a fraction of a second, shifting her book bag from one shoulder to the other. "We can't be late today!" she reminded her friend. "Ms. Rodriguez says she has big news for us this morning in homeroom—remember?"

It was a beautiful fall morning. The trees lining Beacon Street glinted with gold and red. Crisp and clear, the air felt invigorating as the girls hurried together past the bright-colored storefronts on their way to school. Ordinarily Charlotte liked to take her time as she ambled down Beacon Street, which ran beside the trolley tracks leading east into the city. Her walk to school had already become a familiar routine—stopping at Montoya's Bakery for one of their kid-sized blueberry muffins and waving to her new friend Yuri, the Russian man who ran the small grocery store at the corner. He was often outside in the morning rinsing off the stacks of red and green apples in the open cases lining the front of his shop. Sometimes she even had time to stop and check out the new books in the window of her favorite bookstore.

But this morning Charlotte was short on time. First, her alarm hadn't gone off and she'd overslept, thanks to staying up so late writing in her journal. Every attempt to get her hair to look OK failed dismally. One braid kept sticking out like an antenna. Then her shoelaces broke, and the only new ones she could find were magenta. Nice look, she thought wryly, glancing down to see one sneaker with white laces and the other with laces the color of a ripe mango. But thank goodness her vintage jean jacket was just where she left it. That jacket had belonged to Charlotte's mother, and it always gave her good luck—as if nothing bad could happen to her when she was wearing it. Of course, her copy of *To Kill a Mockingbird*, which she needed for English class, was wedged under a pile of laundry on the chair in her bedroom. "Oh well ... Mondays!" Charlotte sighed.

Most days, Charlotte and her dad ate breakfast together before he cycled off to Boston University, where he was teaching writing this semester. They took turns making breakfast. Charlotte loved to cook, especially for her dad, who was the world's most appreciative audience. Her specialty was herbed scrambled eggs with grated French gruyère cheese. If she got up early enough, she could scan the cartoon page of the newspaper and sip hot chocolate while her dad finished his coffee. Not today. This morning Professor Ramsey was running late too. Charlotte was halfway out the door before she remembered that she'd forgotten to kiss Marty—the adorable, floppy-eared dog she and her friends had adopted—good-bye.

"Marty, you are too cute," Charlotte chided him, kissing his head as she scooted him back behind the door. He kept trying to follow her, it took three tries to get him to settle down before she could go. "Marty, I promise, little buddy, we'll have a good long walk when I get home," Charlotte said as she rushed toward the door. By this point Charlotte was in such a state that she almost plowed smack into Sapphire Pierce, the Ramseys' landlady, as she dashed out the door.

Miss Pierce had shaken her head, smiling. "Good morning, Charlotte!" she'd called fondly as Charlotte raced off again like a cyclone. The Ramseys didn't know Miss Pierce at all when they first moved in—she kept to her own apartment on the first floor, and seemed to be almost a recluse. Now, Charlotte and Miss Pierce were beginning to become friends. Miss Pierce used to be an astronomer at the Hubble Observatory before she retired and moved back to Brookline. She loved talking to Charlotte about the stars, and lately they had started having tea together every once in a while in the afternoons. But this morning there was no time for more than a frantic hello.

8:05! Charlotte didn't want to be late, today of all days. Ms. Rodriguez, her homeroom teacher, had promised to share some exciting news with the class this morning. Not that Charlotte could stand to be a minute late anyway. She loved junior high—now that she felt at home there, and now that she had friends to share it with!

It was hard to believe that just a few weeks ago, all of this—Brookline, the Abigail Adams Junior High School, even her new home—had felt so strange and unfamiliar. Because of her dad's career as a travel writer, Charlotte had lived all over the world. Since her mother died, she and her father had been on the move every few years. They were a team—that's what her father always said. Last year they had even gotten to live in a houseboat on the Seine, the river that runs through the heart of Paris. Before that, they'd lived in Port Douglas, Australia—and before that, in the Serengeti desert in Tanzania, Africa. Other kids always marveled at all the places Charlotte had seen. Charlotte never lost the sense of wonder that came with discovering something (or someone) new. But now that she was almost thirteen, staying in one place and having a real home felt more and more important to her.

So this time, when her father let Charlotte pick their destination, she'd chosen Brookline, Massachusetts, just a few miles from downtown Boston where she and her mom and dad had lived when she was a baby.

Charlotte was convinced that this move would be different from any of the others. She was certain that she and her father were going to put down roots this time. After all, they'd found a fabulous house to live in. They were renting the second floor of Miss Pierce's house, 173 Summit Avenue, a beautiful rambling yellow Victorian with a huge front porch, leaded windows, and lots of charm. Inside, the house was filled with nooks and crannies—thick, carved banisters, oak-pegged floors, and high ceilings. Everything about it reminded Charlotte of another era, from the stained-glass window on the landing to the cozy window seats piled with plump cushions. The house sat high on Corey Hill. From the top floors you could see east to the CITGO sign in Kenmore Square and south all the way to the Charles River. Charlotte had her own balcony off her bedroom where she could look at the stars at night. Even better, the top floor of the house led to an amazing cupola with a tower room that you got to by crawling up through a trap door in the ceiling. It was just like a secret hideaway in a novel!

Charlotte and her three best friends had found the Tower by accident during an overnight. Once they'd found it, they'd discovered that it made a perfect BFF hangout. The four of them could escape up to the Tower to read, to study, to play music, to tickle Marty—to do anything they felt like ... Even before they learned that the Tower used to be a special place for Miss Pierce when she was a girl, it still cast its wonderful spell over them. The Tower was an amazing place to get away from the world and to be alone. Charlotte's friends had helped her carry her writing desk up to the Tower attic, and she loved working up there on her stories. It was so high up that Charlotte felt like she was floating above the city. It was a wonderful place for inspiration ... and the perfect place to look at the stars.

Stars and books, Charlotte was thinking, as she and Maeve hurried down Harvard Street. Stars and books had always been her best friends. For the first few weeks at Abigail

Adams Junior High, Charlotte had worried that they were going to be her only friends. It wasn't easy getting to know a whole new bunch of kids. Even though everyone else was new to junior high too, most of them knew kids from elementary school to make it all less terrifying. Not Charlotte. She'd been entirely on her own, until ...

As if on cue, she heard Maeve's voice cutting through her reverie.

"Hey," Maeve gasped. She was a little out of breath from trying to keep up with Charlotte. "Can't we ... save some ... energy for ... when we actually ... get ... there?"

Charlotte grinned, pushing her glasses up with the tip of her finger. "School starts in fifteen minutes," she pointed out. "Remember?"

Maeve hurried beside her, her green eyes sparkling. "My memory doesn't work at this speed," she gasped. "Slow down!"

Charlotte burst out laughing. Maeve packed so much personality into every phrase. Everything she said seemed to have an exclamation point after it! Maeve was stunning, with long red hair tumbling around her shoulders, big green movie-star eyes, and skin the color of soft peaches. Movie star said it all when it came to Maeve's biggest passion in life. She loved anything having to do with movies, new or old. Every inch of her backpack was covered with buttons: movie stars, old and new; a bright colored "Yes!"; an "LOL"; and a big "Hollywood Rocks!" button right in the middle. Maeve loved to dress up, rock star style. Today, she'd added a cool new touch—a long knit scarf swinging back over one shoulder. "Filene's Basement," she confided to Charlotte, tossing it back behind her. "From the five-dollar bin, can you believe it?"

Charlotte laughed, looking affectionately at her friend. Drama wasn't confined to the big screen for Maeve—and bargains weren't the only things she hunted for! Maeve was a real heart-on-her-sleeve girl. At first, this quality had put Charlotte off—she had thought Maeve was boy-crazy. Last month, Maeve had a big crush on Nick Montoya, the easy-going, down-to-earth seventh grader whose family owned Montoya's Bakery. For a while, Maeve talked about Nick all the time. Her friends had heard constantly about how much Maeve liked him—even though it seemed pretty clear that Nick was only interested in Maeve as a friend. Finally, Maeve had summoned up her courage and asked Nick to go see a movie with her a few weeks ago. But their "date"—if you could call it that—had been a total flop. Nick didn't seem to have a romantic bone in his body—at least not where Maeve was concerned.

It hadn't helped matters that Nick actually seemed interested in Charlotte. Charlotte blushed a little, remembering the moment a few weeks back when Nick had bumped into her, walking Marty in the park. Nick wasn't the romantic type—that's what Maeve had complained. But there was something ... Charlotte didn't know what to call it—some kind of little charge whenever Nick was around her. Charlotte could feel it. That time when he'd leaned toward her, as if—

Anyway, she thought, shaking off the memory. The point was, Nick and Maeve—that hadn't worked. Charlotte wasn't going to let herself think about Nick that way. They were good friends, that was all.

One thing that Charlotte really appreciated about Maeve was that she could laugh at herself. She never held a grudge, either. Maeve had gotten over Nick the minute she learned that he didn't like *Gone With the Wind*. "Forget that," she'd confided in her friends. "I'm not spending time with someone who doesn't feel romantic when they watch Scarlett and Rhett kissing!"

In fact, Maeve always seemed to bounce back quickly. Before she'd had time to be upset about Nick, she'd decided she was really interested in Billy, one of the Trentini twins. That hadn't lasted long, either. Not since she had discovered Dillon Johnson, a boy in their homeroom who was every bit as high-spirited as Maeve. Now Dillon was on Maeve's mind every minute of the day and night, and she wasn't exactly shy about expressing her feelings. "I think today Ms. Rodriguez is going to change our desks around," Maeve bubbled over, as she and Charlotte charged up Harvard Street toward their school. "If only she moves me next to Dillon ..." She pretended to swoon.

"Earth to Maeve!" Charlotte chided her. "We have to get to school before we can actually find our desks—remember?"

Despite Maeve's effervescent personality and upbeat humor, she had her share of problems. She had dyslexia, which meant she had to use a laptop in class to take notes, and she had to take all of her quizzes and exams in the Learning Lab. The fact that Maeve's little brother Sam had an IQ of about a million didn't make her life any easier. Her mother also gave her a hard time. Carol worried constantly about Maeve's learning disability. She seemed to think that the best approach was to cram every second of Maeve's life with lessons—she packed her after-school schedule so tightly that Maeve hardly had a spare minute to herself. It took ingenuity, Maeve confided in her friends, to be able to find a second of free time for herself. But Maeve had plenty of ingenuity, so her free time remained a protected (if endangered!) resource.

"So, I have news," Maeve told Charlotte, breathing a little harder as they hurried. "My mom got a call last night from Ms. Fitzgerald—you know, Betsy's mom? She's president of the PTO ..."

She never got to finish her sentence. The two girls were already running up the steps of the Abigail Adams School. Their junior high had two sections—one old, one new. The old yellow brick middle part had stone steps, double front doors, lanterns, a steep roof, and a clock tower—the epitome of old New England. The two newer, low sides pointing toward the street were just big, ugly yellow rectangles. Charlotte and Maeve hurried up to the seventh-grade entrance. As usual, Ruby Fields, the school principal, was greeting kids as they arrived on the front steps. Mrs. Fields was an amazing principal—she went out of her way to get to know each of the students by name. She was a firm believer in school community, and she liked to shake hands and say hello to as many students as she could every morning.

"Hello, Charlotte," she said warmly, her dark eyes smiling as she gave Charlotte's hand a quick squeeze. "Good morning, Maeve. How was your weekend?"

"Ummm ... busy, Ruby ... Oops! I'm sorry. I mean, Mrs. Fields," Maeve said, blushing deeply. Mrs. Fields was their friend Katani Summers' grandmother. "Lots of homework," she added quickly, blushing even more deeply when Mrs. Fields gave her a quizzical smile. When Mrs. Fields's penetrating gaze turned on you, it always felt like she could see straight through you right to your very core!

"Lots of homework—which I didn't do," Maeve added to Charlotte under her breath with a sigh, as they moved away from their principal and into the front lobby of the school. "I mean, I meant to, but it took me forever just to read the first chapter of *To Kill a Mockingbird*. Did you even understand that book?" She giggled. "Thank heavens they made it into a movie!"

Charlotte didn't want to admit that she'd actually read ahead. She loved reading about Scout and Atticus.

"Maeve," Charlotte said gently, as they weaved their way through the crowded front hall of the school. "You shouldn't lie to Mrs. Fields! Anyway, she's the one who likes to remind us that it's important for kids to have fun. She wouldn't want you to spend your whole weekend doing homework."

"I know—but I overdid the fun this weekend," Maeve confessed. "I was helping my parents at the theater, and they got these amazing new movies in that I just had to help them preview, and then of course—" she sighed, "I started IM-ing—and before I knew it ..." She shrugged, smiling. "There went the weekend!" She grabbed Charlotte's arm. "Look—Dillon's over there! Shouldn't we just ..."

Charlotte practically had to yank Maeve by the arm to pull her over to the cluster of seventh-grade lockers. Kids were milling around, opening up their lockers to put away their jackets and books. The inside door of each locker was personalized with stickers, drawings, initials, and pictures. Charlotte's locker, #117, had a mini corkboard inside it, covered with colorful buttons—and photos of: Orangina, the cat she had to leave behind, Sophie, her best friend in Paris, in a silly pose in front of the Eiffel Tower, and Charlotte and her dad in snorkeling gear in Port Douglas. A picture from *Nature* magazine of Orion, the Hunter—one of the few constellations visible from both the Northern and Southern hemispheres. And, of course, a big picture of Marty, his head cocked in his usual adorable way. Across the bottom of the corkboard, Charlotte had posted a sticker from Earth Day that her dad had given her. It said in big green letters, "BE KIND TO THE PLANET—IT'S THE ONLY ONE WE'VE GOT!"

Maeve's locker was on one side of Charlotte's, and Nick Montoya's was on the other. Maeve's locker—notoriously messy—had papers sticking out through the locker's grates on both the top and the bottom. Maeve didn't seem to notice. "Anyway," she was saying cheerfully, twirling her locker combination, "I've got major news. And this doesn't just affect me, either, it affects everyone!"

"*What* affects everyone?" Avery Madden demanded, dashing up with her skateboard tucked under one arm. Avery had only gotten her skateboard a week ago, and already it seemed like an extension of her body. Charlotte smiled, watching Avery and Maeve almost collide in front of their lockers. It was hard to believe two more different girls could be such good friends. Small, dark-haired, and fiercely intense, Avery was energy in motion. You could pretty much guarantee Avery would've spent her whole weekend on the soccer field. She was the top goalie in the seventh grade! You wouldn't ever catch Avery in anything other than her sweats or gym clothes.

Avery was adopted. Her parents were from Boston, but she had been born in Korea. Avery had come to America when she was just a few months old. Now her mom and dad were divorced, so she spent time with her dad mostly on vacations. She and her two older brothers, Scott and Tim, lived with her mother in a big sprawling house in Brookline. Avery was short, not even five feet, but she was amazingly strong and quick. Charlotte loved Avery because she questioned life. She had a keen sense of right and wrong, and was the last kid to accept just anything because someone told her that's how it should be. And she could sometimes blurt out whatever was on her mind. As Maeve liked to point out, sensitivity was not exactly Avery's strong point. *Even so, I bet she'll change the world one day,* Charlotte thought. *But she may step on a few toes along the way!*

Charlotte's father had come up with a great description for Avery. He said she was like a photon, a tiny particle of energy. Charlotte didn't think she'd ever seen Avery sitting still. Avery adored sports and games of all kinds. Put any kind of ball in front of her and she was happy. She loved motion—jumping, gliding, and sliding. If she couldn't be outside, she'd be the first to invent an indoor game to play. She was addicted to cards and was an ace chess player. And ... she was crazy about dogs, particularly Marty. "After all, she was the one to find him."

But Avery had her own issues, too. It wasn't always easy being shuffled back and forth between her mom's house and her dad's home in Colorado. Worse, her mom couldn't understand the fact that Avery would much rather play pickup basketball than go to an art museum or to Symphony Hall. Lately, her mother was on a new crusade to get Avery interested in classical music. She said it stretched the size of your brain. Personally, Avery thought it was boring! Even worse, her father, who was a total sports fanatic, seemed to think that her older brothers were the only ones who would appreciate tickets to a Red Sox game ... And of course, there was the whole girly-girl dress thing with her mother. Life, Avery thought with a sniff, was sometimes the opposite of fair.

"Don't let it bother anyone," Avery said now, stuffing her soccer bag into her locker, "but the homeroom bell's gonna ring in about five seconds." She rolled up her sleeve, squinting down at a message she'd written to herself on her arm. This was a new habit of Avery's—she claimed her arm was the best place for important messages. "Don't forget math homework," she read out loud, reaching back into her locker for another notebook. "I like this system," she added, inspecting the writing on her wrist. "It takes the idea of a Palm Pilot to new levels." She grinned. "Think Ms. Rodriguez would mind if I skated into class?"

Maeve giggled, picturing Avery flying over the desks like the girl on the cover of her skateboard magazine. "You know she'd kill you. 'Skateboards in lockers, please,'" she added, impersonating their favorite teacher.

Avery opened her locker, trying to cram her skateboard inside.

"Avery," Charlotte said, wrinkling her nose, "What on earth have you got in there?" She leaned forward and fished a wad of old gym clothes out of Avery's locker. Laughing, she said, "How can you ever find anything in that mess?"

Avery laughed. "Are you kidding? I've got a whole year's worth of clothes in here. Soccer shorts ... soccer socks ... cleats ... that's all you need, right? This is like having your clothes closet right here at school!"

"Hey, guys!" Katani Summers walked over from her locker. She smiled at Charlotte's expression of horror over Avery's locker. "Avery, I think it's time for one of my famous locker-makeovers. Don't worry. My services are free for friends ... at least the first time." She narrowed her eyes a little. "Although yours looks like quite a challenge," she admitted. She pretended to take a whiff and drew back in horror. "Phew! Maybe some jasmine-scented air-freshener ..."

The girls laughed—even Avery. Katani's design sense

was legendary. Tall and dark-haired, Katani put her own fashion touch on everything she did. She had a great sense of style and a confident personality to match. Some kids thought she could seem a little aloof on occasion, but Katani was a warm and loving friend once you got to know her. She would do absolutely anything for Maeve, Charlotte, or Avery if they really needed her. Ten minutes with her prized sewing machine, her signature vintage fabrics, and some rhinestones, and Katani could pull something together that looked straight off the cover of a magazine. She was that talented! Fashion and business were her two passions. For as long as she could remember, Katani had been saving money from babysitting, and finally saved almost enough to buy a few shares of stock in a company, and she couldn't wait! Katani's mother was going to help her—it was one of her strong beliefs that girls should learn more about business so that they could stand on their own two feet.

Katani lived with two of her three sisters, her mom and dad, and her grandmother, Ruby Fields, the principal of Abigail Adams Junior High. They shared a two-family in Brookline—Katani's mother called it "cozy," but Katani thought it was just plain small. Sharing a room with her sister Kelley meant absolutely no privacy. It also meant she had to be super organized, because Kelley, who was mildly autistic, couldn't keep anything together. The good thing was that Katani loved order, anyway. She kept everything in her bedroom—buttons, shoes, ribbons—all boxed up, labeled, and super neat. Katani *liked* her world that way.

Much as Katani loved *control*, things were far from perfect in her world. Katani did her best to keep her issues to herself—not out of secrecy, but because she really valued privacy, poise, and cool. Katani's older sister Candice, who was away at college, was a hard act to follow—perfect grades, perfect everything—and a star basketball player to boot. Next in the lineup came Patrice, 16, a sophomore this year at Brookline High—and good at every sport (and every activity) she tried. Not to mention popular, pretty, and always right. Patrice didn't exactly keep her talents hidden, either! Conceited, conceited, conceited, was the way Katani would describe her. Not to mention a total bathroom hog. It wasn't easy for Katani to have to explain to people that just because she was a Summers, and despite the fact that she was super tall, she wasn't a star on the basketball court— another sore point with Katani. She couldn't help the fact that she was tall and still growing. She hated more than anything when people commented on her height. "Look how much you've grown!" Katani hated when people said this to her. Didn't they realize that personal comments about a person's body were way out of line?

On the bright side, one of the things that had started Katani sewing in the first place was the fact that she couldn't find blue jeans long enough to fit her. Now, a few extra inches of vintage fabric adorned every pair of her jeans. Katani's friends all begged her to make them some just like hers, which gave Katani a secret feeling of pride. Still, her height continued to bug her—especially since it didn't come with a single bit of athletic skill. It was so painful having to walk every single day past the junior high display case and see her sisters' rows of trophies up there, winking down at her. Candice Summers—Basketball, All Star Soccer, Player of the year. Patrice Summers, Best All-Around Athlete, 3 years running. Blah blah blah! As if to make it even worse, there happened to be a little empty space next to Patrice's trophy— as if to mock Katani. As if the trophies were all saying:

Where's yours? Katani didn't even like sports except for golf which she and her dad had recently discovered, but her sisters thought it was geeky.

Anyway, did it matter that she was a straight A student and a math whiz? Where were the trophies for that? When Candice got a scholarship to UMass, the whole world heard about it. When Patrice made Varsity on every team she tried out for, it always called for a family celebration. But as far as Katani could see, there was no varsity team for fashion design. And no trophies for being good at math and business, either. How unfair was that?

Candice and Patrice were a tough double-act to follow. But they weren't the hardest part for Katani. Katani's sister Kelley, who was in ninth grade, was a much bigger challenge. Having autism could mean different things for different people. For Kelley, it meant that she needed a full-time aide, Ms. Mathers, to help her out in school. Kelley still liked to lug around her favorite stuffed animal, Mr. Bear, even though she was fourteen. She could remember amazing details, but sometimes she couldn't even answer the simplest questions.

Katani adored her sister, though it made her squirm inside when she felt embarrassed by her. Even though she was younger than Kelley by almost two years, Katani had to look out for her at school. It was her job to wait for Kelley after last period and walk her home. Katani had kind of dreaded that about starting junior high. For the past two years, Kelley had been over here at Abigail Adams, and Katani had been able to enjoy fifth and sixth grade without feeling responsible for her sister. It wasn't that she didn't love Kelley—she did! But she couldn't help worrying about what it would mean for her when she started at Abigail Adams, too. Her biggest fear was that someone would pick on Kelley, or make fun of her. She was so glad that Charlotte, Maeve, and Avery accepted her sister for who she was. It was one more reason that she'd do anything for her friends—absolutely anything.

Even fix up Avery's locker!

But Avery had no interest in any makeovers of any kind. The word "makeover" grated on her like nails on a blackboard. She slammed her locker door shut. "Not on my life," she muttered. "Don't you dare redo any part of me, Katani. Not my locker." She caught sight of Katani's gaze, lighting on her pig-tailed hair. "And not the rest of me either!"

She didn't mean to say it quite as strongly as she did. But that was Avery for you. Always a few decibels louder than anyone else. And definitely not shy about her feelings!

THINKING BACK

Listening to her friends tease each other, Charlotte felt a wave of happiness wash over her. It was hard to believe she hadn't known them forever. She could still remember how it had felt on Day One, walking down Harvard Street, butterflies in her stomach, hoping—for once—that she could manage to pull off a first day at a new school without managing to totally embarrass herself. Now, looking back on it, it seemed funny. But it sure hadn't felt funny then.

"What are you smiling about?" Maeve demanded, linking arms as they started down the hall to Ms. Rodriguez's homeroom. "I haven't even told you my fabulous news yet!"

"I was just remembering the first day of school," Charlotte told her.

Katani fell into step beside them. "Please," she groaned. "I can't even think about it." She pretended to shudder and pulled her beautiful red knit sweater a little closer to her—

and further away from Charlotte. Charlotte had to laugh. Ms. Rodriguez, the girls' homeroom and English teacher, had stuck the four of them together in what she had optimistically referred to as a "lunch group." She'd thought it would be a good icebreaker to assign kids to lunch tables, since the whole seventh grade was new to Abigail Adams. Only no one else was as new as Charlotte was. And nobody else had the Charlotte klutz-factor either, Charlotte thought ruefully. How was it humanly possible to zip a tablecloth into her jeans and pull it out from under four lunch trays? And how had it just happened that the disgustingly sticky French toast sticks she'd bought for lunch that day had to land, syrup and all, on top of Katani's gorgeous Pucci-style top? Charlotte didn't even know at the time that Katani was a designer extraordinaire and had spent all of August and lots of babysitting money on the silk shirt she was wearing that day. What a disaster!

"That's all behind us," Maeve said chummily. "Remember—we're the Beacon Street Girls now!"

The Beacon Street Girls was the name the four girls—Charlotte, Maeve, Katani, and Avery—had inherited from their hideaway in the Tower room. They'd found the Tower by accident—or by magic, depending on how you looked at it. In a way, finding the Tower was Ms. Rodriguez's doing, too. Because after their lunch group had turned out to be such a dismal failure, Katani had convinced Ms. Rodriguez to give the four girls this unusual assignment: Get together for a one-night sleepover, and if they still couldn't get along, then they could go their separate ways.

Every time Charlotte thought about that first sleepover she felt a rush of emotion. She could still remember how much she'd dreaded the event, and how awkward it had been at the beginning ... her dad all excited that she finally had "friends" coming over and refusing to listen when Charlotte kept telling him they were only coming because they had to. And how weird it felt sitting around, sipping hot chocolate and waiting for *someone* to say something. Finally, when the four girls were getting ready for bed, this whole huge fight had erupted, with everyone yelling at everyone ... Katani furious with Charlotte for wrecking her favorite outfit, and Maeve exploding at Katani for accusing her of being spoiled rotten, and Avery mad at Katani for sounding like she was *dissing* adoption ... which she wasn't, and the next thing the girls knew, they were all pouring their hearts out to each other. Really talking about who they were, what they feared and worried about, and how they really felt.

When Charlotte looked at the other girls now, it was hard to believe that four such different girls could become so close. But in many ways, the differences between them were the best part of their friendship. Together they were ... how did Mr. Sherman in pre-algebra put it? ... Together they were more than the sum of their parts!

"Hey—you still haven't let me tell you my news," Maeve reminded Charlotte. She twirled around dramatically, pulling a printed invitation out of her velvet book bag. "Look what my mom gave me last night. She got hers early because she's on the Arts Committee. You guys should be getting one any day."

Seventh-Grade Social Dancing

Learn classical dance steps!
Practice manners and social graces!
Free dancing too!
Sponsored by the PTO

Brookline Neighborhood Club
Wednesday evenings, 7-9 P.M.
Attire: Dressy

"You've got to be kidding," Avery said, scowling. "You call this *good* news?"

"It's not every Wednesday," Maeve said quickly, "just once a month. It sounds amazing. There's going to be refreshments ... and they're going to teach us how to do cool new dances, and the classics." She bounced a little, her eyes shining with excitement. "And at the end of every class, there's a chance for the guys to ask the girls to dance—and then the other way around. Girls' choice!"

"Let's guess," Avery said dryly. "Who do you think Maeve might pick? Hold on," she added. "The suspense is killing me."

"Hmm," Katani said, eyeing the card. "I like the sound of 'dressy attire.' Sounds like a perfect opportunity for someone with a designer's eye ... Moi, for instance."

"My mom says everyone on the PTO is completely behind this. They're all going to make their kids do it. Even all the guys!" Maeve sang out happily. She hugged herself. "She's pretty sure Dillon's mom is going to send him. Same for Pete Wexler. And Nick! And the Trentini twins." She was practically spinning with joy. "I can just see it now. It'll be like the big waltz at the end of *My Fair Lady*, when Audrey Hepburn dances with everyone and her neck is so long and graceful that no one can tell she isn't a princess!"

"Give me a break," Avery snorted. "This is so not like that, Maeve. Can't you see this is just a grown-up plot to shove us all into a room and make us civilized?"

Charlotte peered anxiously at the announcement. She had a completely different worry. If a person can't even manage to get through a school cafeteria without humiliating herself publicly, how on earth could that same person be expected to survive a *dance class*? Dancing was not exactly Charlotte's thing—not even the kind of dancing where you just got up and moved around to the music, let alone something like this, where you had to get the steps right! As a self-professed klutz, Charlotte had to admit she was on Avery's side on this one. Katani and Maeve, however, gave each other a high-five, looking like they'd just won the lottery.

"I think off-the-shoulder," Katani advised, her arm around Maeve's shoulder. "And colors—we have to think of something very this year." She thought for a minute. "Mulberry," she added. "Or maybe aubergine." Katani so loved exotic names for colors. Yellow, her favorite, she liked to refer to as "Tuscan gold."

"Dillon," Maeve breathed rapturously. "Just think, I'm going to have at least one Wednesday evening a month where I can get Dillon to ask me to dance!" She paused. "And a chance to ask him, too. It's going to be heaven!"

Charlotte shook her head as the four girls crowded

together into homeroom, just as the last bell rang. This didn't sound like such good news to her. She hoped whatever Ms. Rodriguez had in store for them was going to be better than this!

CHAPTER 2

❦

CHANGING THE RULES

MS. RODRIGUEZ had her "even though it's Monday morning, I'm still in a good mood" look on her face. There was the usual mad scramble to get into homeroom before the P.A. system blared morning announcements. Today there was more confusion than usual, since all the students had new places—which meant extra time was not only needed for wandering around to find their seats, but for commenting on the new arrangement. The announcements began before they were all settled, and Maeve groaned. "We definitely need music," she muttered. "Don't you know they've done studies on this? Kids our age are *much* more responsive if they hear something with a good beat before getting down to work." She'd found her new desk and was trying to cram her bag into it without much luck. She finally gave up and pulled out her laptop, it was a special privilege because of her trouble with spelling and writing, but not much of a pleasure as far as Maeve was concerned.

Ms. Rodriguez kept a seating chart. She had used it the first few weeks of class so she could get to know everyone and everyone could get to know each other. Now she rotated seats every few weeks so nobody would "get in a rut." Today's assignment landed Charlotte between Dillon Johnson and Betsy Fitzgerald. "Omigod," Maeve hissed when she saw Charlotte slide into her seat next to Dillon. "Charlotte Ramsey, this is the most unfair thing ever!" Maeve was way over on the other side of the room, next to Riley Lee, who wore his dark, unruly hair long and played bass guitar. There weren't that many guys who Maeve didn't think had crush potential, but Riley was definitely off her list. "Way too into the grunge thing, which is so over," she'd described him to Charlotte. "And what's with the all-black clothing thing? *Gross!*"

Charlotte would've been willing to trade seats with Maeve if she could—she could tell her friend was absolutely dying to be next to Dillon. But they all had to respect Ms. Rodriguez's new assignments.

TYPE A+

Betsy Fitzgerald had her "Student Planner" out and was thumbing through it. She had every day organized with three different color pens—assignments in blue, tests in green, and long-term projects in red. "Big math test this week," she announced, to nobody in particular. "I hope everybody's planning for it." She frowned a little, squinting at the planner. "Oh, and we have our first major paper due in social studies on Friday, too!"

"Please," Dillon groaned. "Betsy, is there such a thing as a type A+? Or are you just obsessive-compulsive? It's too early in the morning to worry about things like tests and papers."

Betsy blinked at him. "You know, Dillon, I happen to like a little organization in my life, OK?" She sat up straight and smoothed her hair back. Not that there was anything to smooth back—she had every hair in place under her tidy headband. She folded her hands and gave Dillon a prim, disapproving look. Everything about Betsy always looked like it had just come from the dry cleaner. Perfect.

Ms. Rodriguez cleared her throat. "Did everyone have a good weekend?"

Anna McMasters and Joline Kaminsky, Abigail Adams Junior High's resident "Queens of Mean," gave each other significant looks. Joline leaned over to whisper something to Anna and they both giggled.

"Something you'd like to share with the rest of us, Joline?" Ms. Rodriguez asked pleasantly.

Joline kept a deadpan cool look on her face without flinching. Charlotte glanced at her wonderingly. How did Joline do that—manage to look so scornful without even rolling her eyes? It was pretty amazing if you didn't let it get to you personally. At every school Charlotte had ever attended, there'd been someone like Joline. Someone with *superior* written all over her face, and a way of cutting you down without saying a single word. How did you even get to be that way? Charlotte wondered. Was it hard-wired? Or was it somehow contagious? "The Whisperers," she and Sophie had called them in Paris. Even before Charlotte's French was good enough to understand, she could pick them out. It was that certain combination of snobbery and power ... a universal language.

"No thanks, Ms. Rodriguez," Joline murmured silkily. But the look she shot back to Anna said it all. They'd probably gone together to some exclusive high school party, Charlotte thought. Or more likely, they sneaked into an "R" movie with some of the eighth and ninth graders they liked hanging out with. Sometimes she thought Anna and Joline didn't even need actual language, since they had the body language thing down so well.

One shoulder turned in meant: Don't you dare sit with us.

One lifted eyebrow meant: You are so juvenile.

Direct eye contact with each other meant: The two of us are the coolest things that walk the earth. Other mortals— stay away!

One derisive snort of laughter means: That was an inside joke. And you are *so* on the outside!

Anna and Joline intimidated just about everybody with their super-cool, "we're so in and you're so not" kind of attitude. It was funny, though—Anna and Joline didn't seem to have as much fun together as Charlotte and her friends did.

Ms. Rodriguez was still interested in hearing about people's weekends.

Pete Wexler's hand went up. The J.V. football team won their game, he announced, 24 to 7.

Other people mentioned things. Nick Montoya had gone hiking in the Blue Hills in Milton. Avery had everyone laughing when she described doing double ollies over some chairs in her driveway and almost breaking her arm. Samantha Simmons, who loved dropping hints to remind everyone that her family was incredibly wealthy, described driving down to Cape Cod to their second home. "We had to take our new ski boat out of the water for the winter," she announced, which prompted some serious eye rolling from Anna and Joline.

Dillon, who was obsessed with action movies, took almost five minutes telling everyone the plot of the latest fantasy movie he'd seen—until Ms. Rodriguez cut him short. "That sounds very exciting, Dillon," she said with a smile, "but I think we need to give others a chance—"

Betsy's hand shot up. "My weekend was excellent. I signed up at a test-prep center to get coaching on the PSATs." She glanced around the room, waiting for a reaction, and when none came, she added, "You know, you can raise your scores by quite a few points if you just take the time to prepare."

Dillon coughed and Ms. Rodriguez shot him a look. "Well. That certainly sounds like you're thinking ahead, Betsy," she said. Trust Ms. Rodriguez to find something encouraging to say—even to Betsy.

Anna and Joline exchanged a superior smirk. Betsy drove them up a wall and they didn't exactly hide it. They were still dumfounded by the fact that Betsy actually argued with Mr. Sherman when she got a 98 on her most recent math test. She wanted 100 percent, and she kept trying to prove to him that the one error she'd made wasn't an error after all.

Betsy wasn't done yet. "I *liked* the prep class. It's really important to think ahead. It's not too soon to start thinking about applying to college. *My* brother, who goes to Harvard, always says ..."

Anna snorted, and then tried to cover it with a sneeze. A bunch of people giggled.

Ms. Rodriguez's eyebrows shot up. Betsy was very fond of quoting her older brother, who was a sophomore at Harvard. The class had already heard quite a few of his views on getting into the best colleges.

"College!" Dillon shrieked. "We're in *seventh grade!* Give me a break."

Fortunately Ms. Rodriguez was already calling on someone else. Abby Ross, a friendly, round-faced girl who sat in the back row, talked about the walk she'd gone on to raise money for Project Bread, an organization that brought in money to buy food for people who needed it.

Betsy's hand shot back up. "That's so great, Abby, " she said. "That sort of thing looks really good when you apply to schools. My brother says—"

"Betsy," Ms. Rodriguez cut in. "I think Abby was trying to tell us about her experience. Please, let's listen—and give her a chance."

"Anyway," Abby Ross added, "it's not exactly a good thing if you help people and use it to your own advantage."

Betsy frowned. "I don't see why not," she objected. "People can still get their food. And you can get credit for it. So everyone wins." Betsy always saw the pragmatic side. But, as Avery put it, Betsy's favorite subject was always really "How Can Betsy Get Ahead?"

"You raise an interesting point," Ms. Rodriguez said. "Doing something helpful, and wanting credit for it ..." She looked thoughtful. "I think Abby's raised something worth thinking about. You know, adults struggle with these issues, too. When we do something to help someone, shouldn't that be the primary goal?"

Betsy looked a little miffed, but Charlotte thought Ms. Rodriguez was right. She thought of her favorite character of all times, Charlotte in the book *Charlotte's Web*. Charlotte didn't ask for credit when she saved Wilbur's life, did she? In fact, she refused to be considered a hero. She worked her magic selflessly—out of love. *If I ever do anything to help someone, that's how I would want to do it,* Charlotte thought to herself.

That was the best thing about Ms. Rodriguez's homeroom. The students really had a chance to talk about things that mattered. But today, discussion got cut short.

"This gives us a lot to think about, but today, we have some important business to discuss—as I mentioned in class on Friday," Ms. Rodriguez said. She smiled. "You may remember that for the past few weeks I've been asking you to write letters to me suggesting school rules that you'd like to see changed. I have been trying my best to see what we can do about acting on some of them."

"Yay! More school dances!" Dillon called out. It was no mystery that Dillon had asked for more seventh-grade dances. Across the room, Maeve beamed, taking Dillon's suggestion as a personal compliment.

Ms. Rodriguez shook her head at him. "I said, SOME of the rules," she emphasized. "In fact, I'm happy to be able to report this morning that one school rule has been changed— thanks to a suggestion from Charlotte Ramsey." She smiled in Charlotte's direction. Charlotte sat up a little straighter. She couldn't believe her ears.

"You all know that for years, *The Sentinel*—our school newspaper—has been staffed by eighth and ninth graders. Charlotte wondered in her Change a School Rule Letter why seventh graders couldn't write for the paper as well. I did some investigating, and it turns out that this particular rule was something that had been put in place ages ago. And since nobody really questioned it, it just stayed in place. That sometimes happens, which is one reason why it's so important to keep questioning rules—and to work on changing the ones that don't make sense. So, this morning, Jennifer Robinson, the editor-in-chief of *The Sentinel*, has handed me an announcement to share with all of you. In fact, the whole seventh grade is learning about this today."

Ms. Rodriguez read the announcement from an email

she'd printed out. "Any seventh grader who would like to write for *The Sentinel* should submit a brief writing sample by next Friday. We'd love your involvement, so please submit your best work!"

Charlotte's heart started to beat a little faster. She couldn't imagine anything she'd like better than the chance to write for *The Sentinel*. She'd always wanted to be a writer for as long as she could remember. She couldn't believe her "change a rule" letter had actually made a difference! She felt so pleased and excited. She was hoping Ms. Rodriguez would go on and say a bit more about the writing sample that the editorial staff had asked for, but just then the homeroom door opened and Mrs. Fields slipped her head in. "Ms. Rodriguez? I hate to interrupt, but I wanted to let you know that your new student, Isabel Martinez, is here."

Ms. Rodriguez nodded. Everyone craned heads. Mrs. Fields came into the room, followed by a pretty girl with soft caramel-colored eyes and beautiful, raven black hair cascading down her back. She was wearing fashionably tight jeans and a white V-neck T-shirt which looked great on her curvy figure. There was a sparkle in her eyes, but she looked slightly shy, too.

"Class," Mrs. Fields said, "this is Isabel Martinez. She's just moved here from Michigan. I hope you'll all really make her feel at home."

Charlotte's heart went out to Isabel. All the memories of being new came flooding back. At least she'd never had to start school after it already started! She was so glad that it wasn't her standing in front of the room, looking awkwardly around at the rows of curious faces. But she couldn't help noticing how poised and calm and graceful Isabel seemed. If she was suffering from any first-day pangs, she sure didn't show it. Charlotte guessed that this girl was unlikely to have a first-day disaster. She didn't look at all likely to zip a tablecloth into her jeans and walk off with everyone's lunch trays!

"Isabel, why don't you take a seat behind Charlotte?" Ms. Rodriguez said, pointing to the one empty desk in the room.

Isabel nodded. She walked down the aisle. Even though she moved slowly she had a little bounce in her step. Everybody was trying not to stare at her, but at the same time, it was exciting to have another new classmate.

"Welcome," Ms. Rodriguez said, smiling straight at Isabel. The thing about Ms. Rodriguez was that when she said *welcome*, you can tell that she really means it.

Charlotte was keenly aware of Isabel behind her for the rest of the hour. She couldn't wait to introduce herself. She soon got her chance.

CHAPTER 3

☙

THE FIFTH WHEEL

KATANI WAS very late to lunch. She'd gotten a note from Ms. Mathers saying that Kelley needed her. Mr. Bear, Kelley's favorite stuffed animal—her "transitional object," as Ms. Mathers put it—had gotten lost somehow, and Kelley was dangerously close to a meltdown when Katani found her in the Resource Center. By 12:15, Mr. Bear had been found, and Katani was walking her sister—calmer now, but still sniffling—to the lunchroom. Katani still had her mind on her sister, and barely noticed Maeve charging after them.

"Katani! Kelley! Hey, guys." She fell into step beside them. "Guess what?"

Every other word out of Maeve's mouth was "guess what?" Katani loved Maeve to death, but sometimes she could swear her batteries were overcharged!

"Guess what?" Kelley repeated. Katani could've hugged her. Kelley always seemed to guess exactly what Katani was thinking or feeling.

"Don't forget we were talking a little while ago about making blankets" Maeve said, her eyes sparkling.

"You were talking about it," Katani reminded her wryly. It had happened the night of Maeve's disaster date with Nick. The girls had spent hours helping Maeve to get ready. Katani herself had given Maeve a fabulous makeover. Wasted, all wasted, she thought now, with a sigh. When it was clear that Nick had absolutely no romantic interest in Maeve whatsoever, she'd run back from the Movie House in tears, finding her friends waiting for her up in the Tower room. Somehow, Maeve's darkest hour had given way to a burst of generosity. Maeve had wrapped herself up in a snuggly blanket, and had started wondering, almost out of nowhere, what it would like to be cold and lonely. That was how her idea for making blankets for the homeless had started. Everyone else, as Katani reminded her now, had only listened. It was all Maeve's idea.

Maeve brushed this detail aside. "Anyhow," she hurried on. "My mom and I were talking last night when I was doing my Hebrew homework about the whole idea of 'mitzvahs.'"

"What's that—mitzvah?" Kelley asked. She said it again a few times, obviously liking the word. "Mitz-vah. Mitzzzz-vah."

"It's Hebrew for a 'good thing.' And part of preparing for your Bat Mitzvah is doing something good. You know, thinking about other people, what they need instead of you."

"Like what Betsy said about Abby's Project Bread walk?" Katani said dryly.

Maeve blushed. "The point isn't to talk about it. The point is to do it. Remember our New Tower Rules? Do something to make the world better. You know, like the Miss Rumphius story."

Katani nodded slowly. The New Tower Rules were important to all of them. They'd made up a kind of creed together about things that mattered most to them—like being yourself, treating people fairly, being honest, giving back, taking care of the earth. The New Tower Rules were incredibly special to them. They made them Beacon Street Girls!

Maeve kept going. "Anyway, I was talking to my dad about the blanket thing, and he thought it was a really nice idea." She paused. "My mom wasn't so sure at first, but my dad and I kind of talked her into it. Anyway, she's going to take me to get some fabric today and—" Maeve hesitated, shooting a look at Katani, "And ... well ... you know so much about fabric and stuff—I just thought ..."

Katani sighed. "Maeve, do you need help? Is that what you're saying?"

Maeve threw her arms around her. "Katani, you are the greatest!" she cried. "I knew you'd help me! I just knew it! You are a complete and total sewing, fashion goddess and I adore you!"

Katani stared at her. "I'm a—what?" She shook her head. "Oh, Maeve, I don't know if I ..."

But it was too late. Maeve was already bounding off in the direction of the cafeteria, and it looked like somehow Katani had gotten roped into helping her out.

PULL UP A CHAIR

The Abigail Adams cafeteria was buzzing, as always. Kids were everywhere—crowding around the big round tables; standing in line to buy pizza, burgers, or sandwiches; helping themselves to food from the salad bar; or filling up drinks from the machine at the back of the room. On nice days, kids spilled over into the courtyard outside, sitting on the stone steps or even out on the lawn. Today, since the temperature had dropped, almost everybody was inside. The place looked like a beehive.

Charlotte, Katani, Avery, and Maeve found themselves at their usual table. It was hard to believe that they'd first sat together because they had to—thanks to Ms. Rodriguez's assignment. Now, they couldn't imagine sitting anywhere else.

"What's that?" Katani asked Avery suspiciously, as Avery started to unwrap what appeared to be an enormous submarine sandwich.

Charlotte giggled. Avery's appetite was legendary.

"It's a power sub. Ham, turkey, tomato and lettuce and my favorite new spread—mayo and mustard mixed together." Avery took a huge bite and patted her stomach with great satisfaction, barely noticing the mustard dripping from the end of the sandwich. "This ought to give me enough energy to skateboard home." Her brown eyes fell disapprovingly on Maeve's salad.

"How can you even call that lunch? It looks like guinea pig food," she objected, in characteristic Avery-style—less tactful than honest.

"My guinea pigs do not eat salad," Maeve retorted. Maeve had two guinea pigs—both female—that she liked to pretend were male and female so she could give them romantic names. This week, she was calling them Scarlett and Rhett ... last week it was Lucy and Ricky.

The girls' lunches were as individual as they were. Katani liked to bring delicious things from home, packed with care in bright-colored plastic containers. Maeve was a salad girl. Charlotte stuck to sandwiches or helped herself from the lunch line. Avery was the one with the appetite on steroids!

"No one as small as you are should eat so much," Katani told Avery. "It doesn't make sense."

"I eat like a bird," Avery told her. "Did you know birds

eat more per gram of bodyweight than elephants?" She pointed her sandwich in Katani's direction to demonstrate that most of it was already gone.

Maeve was trying to snitch one of Charlotte's French fries when Ms. Rodriguez came over, just a few steps ahead of Isabel. "Hello girls!" she said warmly, ushering Isabel over to their table. "I've been telling Isabel what great luck I had when I assigned you all to be lunch partners, and I've suggested that she join you at your table today."

Charlotte could feel Avery kicking her leg under the table.

"Please," Ms. Rodriguez added, "make her feel especially welcome." Her voice was warm, but she didn't give them a chance to object. Her eyes moved from one girl to the next with a meaningful expression in them. "Isabel," she added. "Pull up a chair."

Then she was gone, leaving Isabel looking slightly awkwardly around the table at the four of them. She held onto the chair but didn't sit down. "I need to go get something to eat," she said finally. "I'll be right back." She didn't sound exactly shy, just a little tentative.

"OK," the four girls said in unison, with Charlotte adding, "Great!" to make their welcome seem a little warmer.

"Terrific," Katani muttered. "Hasn't Ms. Rodriguez ever heard of the expression 'the fifth wheel'? Can't she see we're doing great just as we are, the four of us?"

"That's not very nice, Katani," Maeve objected. "It's Isabel's very first day here! How would you like showing up in the middle of the grading period and not having anyone to eat lunch with?"

Katani raised her eyebrows and shrugged. She didn't look happy.

Avery talked through a mouthful of food. "I don't really

care," she said philosophically. "But here's a question—if she eats with us today, aren't we going to be stuck with her?" She crammed in the last bit of sandwich. "You think she's going to want to hang out with us all the time? Come up to the Tower and stuff?"

"SSShhhh!!" Maeve turned pink. "She might hear!"

Katani frowned. "Avery's question is good," she said slowly. "Not that I don't want to be friendly or anything, but ... I don't know, we just have a special chemistry, the four of us. I don't want to wreck that! What's it going to be like if all of a sudden we're not four, but five? Maybe things won't be the same."

Maeve tossed back her hair. "Katani, we're best friends, but can't we be nice to someone who's new?! Remember, Charlotte was new and now she's one of our best friends. Besides, just 'cause she's eating with us today doesn't mean she's going to sit with us for the rest of her life. It's just like this wonderful movie I saw once with my dad when Doris Day is new to the city and she moves in with these people she doesn't know and ..."

"Maeve!" Avery groaned. "This is so not the movies."

"The point is," Katani said, "we don't even know her. I mean, she could be perfectly nice, but on the other hand ..."

"Hey, guys," Charlotte said, trying to sound soothing. "There's nothing wrong with being friendly and helping Isabel feel welcome. Let's just give her a chance, OK?"

Katani poked at her chicken casserole. "I still don't see why Ms. Rodriguez couldn't have asked somebody else. Like Betsy Fitzgerald. She could put it on her resume."

"Very funny, Katani," Charlotte laughed.

"SSShhh!" Maeve said again, more emphatically this time. "She's coming back here, Katani! You have to be nice!"

"See," Katani glowered. "She hasn't even sat down yet and she's already ruining everything!"

Isabel made her way back over to the table, balancing a tray in one hand and her backpack in the other. She looked uncertainly around at the four girls before sliding into an empty chair at the end of the table near Maeve and Charlotte.

Maeve sat up a little straighter, a theatrical look on her face. "Isabel," she said, her green eyes fixed on the new girl, "I'm Maeve Kaplan-Taylor." She put out one hand and Charlotte had to suppress a giggle; sometimes Maeve really sounded like she was accepting a Golden Globe award. "And this is Charlotte Ramsey, Katani Summers, and Avery Madden ..." Avery grunted through the last bite of her sandwich. Clearly, Isabel was getting the usual from Avery — no frills.

"You guys are so sweet to let me come and sit with you," Isabel said, pulling her dark hair back with one hand and looking earnestly around the table at them all. "I was really dreading lunch. It's so weird not knowing anyone. But you guys are great—thanks!"

Katani dropped her eyes, embarrassed. But Avery wouldn't know *embarrassed* if she tripped over it.

"So what made you move in the middle of the year?" she asked Isabel bluntly.

That was Avery, Charlotte thought. Like a bull in a china closet!

Isabel didn't seem to mind the question. "Oh—my mom's been having some medical problems," she said simply, "and my aunt, who's a nurse here in Boston, convinced her that we should come up here for a little while so she can have some tests, and maybe some treatment."

Now Katani really looked embarrassed. "Oh. That's

hard," she said. Medical stuff—that made her think at once of Kelley. If Isabel was going through something like that ...

But Isabel clearly didn't want sympathy. "She's going to be fine," Isabel said matter-of-factly. "It's just that the doctors up here are so great, and my Aunt Lourdes is so well-connected. My dad had to stay back in Detroit, so it's just my mom, my older sister, and me for now."

"Wasn't it awfully hard, leaving school right in the middle of the year?" Charlotte asked with compassion.

Isabel shrugged. She seemed like the kind of girl that made the best of everything. "I don't mind," she said with a smile. She had braces with little aqua bands, but that didn't detract from her beauty one little bit. "To tell you the truth, it's kind of exciting to be in a new place." She was pretty open and chatty. Soon she had told the girls all about life back in Detroit—her big, extended family, who had moved up to Detroit two generations ago from Mexico City, with lots of cousins and aunts and uncles, all of them very close. Her mom had always worked as an accountant with her father, and they ran a small accounting firm together, doing people's taxes. Now that she was having health problems, she had to take some time away from work. While her mom was up in Boston, her father would have to run the business all on his own, so he wouldn't be able to visit as much as he would like to. Isabel's older sister, Elena Maria, had started school today, as well, at Abigail Adams—she was in ninth grade. It was much harder for Elena Maria, Isabel confided, because she had to leave her boyfriend Johnny behind in Detroit. "She's pretty upset," Isabel added with a sigh. "So it's kind of up to me to try and cheer her and my mom up a little, if I can."

Maeve couldn't seem to get enough of this information. "Boy, you're so easy to talk to," she told Isabel delightedly.

"You just open right up about stuff!"

Yeah, Katani thought glumly. Isabel was a little too open for Katani's liking. Wasn't it a little too soon to be telling them all this private stuff?

The rest of the lunch period flew by, with Maeve and Charlotte shooting questions at Isabel and Isabel answering, rapid-fire. It was like a prime-time interview. It turned out that Isabel loved to read, just like Charlotte. She loved movies, like Maeve. But her very favorite thing of all was art. "I definitely want to be an artist when I grow up," she told them. "I love painting—and I love drawing comics and cartoons— but my favorite of all is collage-art—I love making special little boxes for my friends." She smiled shyly, looking around the table. "Maybe I can show you guys some stuff I've done."

Maeve bubbled over with excitement at this, but Charlotte noticed that Katani was getting quieter and quieter, poking at her lunch without even tasting it. Come to think of it, Katani had barely said two words to Isabel all through lunch.

ANOTHER PAIR OF HANDS

"Hey," Maeve said, staring at Isabel as if she'd just had the best idea on earth. "If you're artistic, you might want to help me out with my fabulous custom-made blanket idea!" She started describing the project with great enthusiasm, barely noticing how quiet Katani was across the table.

"That sounds wonderful! I'd love to help," Isabel declared.

"Omigod!" Maeve looked like she'd just won the lottery. "We're actually all going fabric shopping this afternoon—me and Katani and my mom," Maeve went on, completely oblivious to Katani's obvious discomfort. "Why don't you come with us, Isabel?"

❁

"I'd have to check first with my mom and my aunt," Isabel began. She glanced a little uncertainly at Katani, who was sending dagger-like looks at Maeve.

"No problem. Check with them, and meet us out front after the last bell!" Maeve sang out. Clearly she couldn't be happier with the idea.

Suddenly Katani got up, pushing her food away with distaste. "I just remembered—I have to pick something up before math next period. See you guys later, OK?"

"I'll come with you," Avery said, jumping up and grabbing her skateboard, with barely a nod back in their direction for good-bye.

Charlotte watched them take off, feeling a little uneasy as Maeve and Isabel continued to chatter together. What was it that Avery and Katani had been saying before Isabel joined their lunch table—that they had such a great thing together, the four of them, and someone new could wreck all of that? She couldn't put her finger on what had just happened, but she could tell that Katani hadn't felt comfortable during lunch. And somehow, the friendlier Maeve was to Isabel, the more withdrawn Katani seemed to become.

Charlotte hoped everything was OK, but she had the definite impression that something was up. It was clear that Katani wasn't as excited about Isabel as Maeve was. Charlotte had seen firsthand what happened when Maeve and Katani clashed, and she just hoped there wasn't going to be trouble between those two again!

Maeve
Notes to Self:

Love my computer and spell checker!

1. Blankets!!!! Must make them cute.
   Happy that Isabel will help!!
   Yay, Katani—she's the magishun.
2. New dres for Social Dancing.
   Blue or green?—both great for
   my eyes. Dillon is so not goin
   to ask anyone to dance but ME.
3. Money-makeing ideas: Mother's
   helper? Who do I know who's got
   kids younger than me who need
   help? Friends of Sam? Too gross.
   Scratch that.
4. Math test coming up—ugghh. Get
   tutor to help.
5. Change I.M. away message to: "Out to
   lunch. If not back by 5, out to
   dinner." Get Dillon's screen name.
6. Countdown to my birthday—
   107 days!!!

Oops! No time for spell check.

CHAPTER 4

☙

THREE'S A CROWD

Katani:
Today's Horoscope

Don't let your friends misunderstand you. You're not fussy, you're a perfectionist! The Virgo girl is thoughtful, intelligent, and has fabulous taste. Your astro challenge: taking risks, listening to your inner voice and making your dreams come true. Believe in yourself!

You may be asked to take a leadership role at school. Speak up! The stars are in your favor this month. Lucky day for love: the 12th.

Unwise day for new business ventures. Begin new projects with caution.

Beware of strangers. They may not have your heart or your trust.

The last thing Katani wanted to do was to meet Maeve and Isabel after school and get dragged along to Fabric World with them. She should've listened to what her star-sign told her, she thought later. She would have been a whole lot better off. This was not a good day to start a new business venture.

"Where are we going, Katani?" Kelley asked thoughtfully, looking concerned. The two girls were standing out in front of the school building, and Katani was wracking her brains, trying to come up with a good excuse to get out of the excursion.

"*We're* not going anywhere," Katani told her sister. She said it more sharply than she'd intended, and a shadow crossed over Kelley's face. She always sensed when her younger sister was upset.

"We're not? We're not going anywhere?" she echoed unhappily.

"No—I mean, yes," Katani mumbled unhappily. "I mean, I don't really want to go, but Maeve needs me, and ..."

"Katani! Over here!" Maeve boomed from the other side of the building. The next minute she came bounding up, her backpack bouncing behind her. "My mom's parked over there," she crowed happily, pointing to the lot behind the school. "And Isabel's going to join us in a second! She's just calling her mom."

Great, Katani thought. Maeve made it sound like the Queen had decided to join them.

"Katani doesn't want to go," Kelley blurted out, taking her sister by the arm.

Katani could feel herself blushing furiously. "I do so, Kelley. Don't say that," she admonished.

That was the thing with Kelley, though. You couldn't get her to lie for anything. "But you said you didn't want to," she protested.

Maeve stared from Kelley to Katani and back again. "Katani," she cried. "What do you mean, you don't want to come? Are you kidding me?"

Katani was feeling worse and worse. "I ... oh, never mind. I said I'd help, so I'll help," she said finally. She gave Kelley a quick hug. "Go in and find Grandma," she told her sister. "And tell her I'll be home before dinner, OK?"

Maeve linked arms with Katani, leading her around to the back parking lot, and chattering obliviously away about how much fun they were all going to have, and how fabulous it was to have Katani and Isabel to help her. She didn't even notice that Katani was clamming up again. That was the thing about Maeve. Sometimes, when she got an idea in her head, she didn't notice much else around her.

"Hello, Katani," Ms. Kaplan said in the concerned parent's voice she used whenever she was talking to one of Maeve's friends. She was in the front seat of her blue Taurus station wagon. Maeve hopped in the front, leaving Katani to slide in next to Isabel.

"Hey," Isabel said with a warm smile.

Katani nodded stiffly back at her. She had no good reason not to like Isabel—she seemed perfectly nice, Katani had to admit. And she liked art, they had that in common. But somehow, some way, she made Katani feel kind of ... invaded. It's like she was going to steal Maeve and make everything weird between all of us, she thought miserably.

It didn't help that Maeve kept up a running conversation with Isabel the entire way to Fabric World. And Isabel had this way of leaning forward, putting her hands on the back of Maeve's seat, so it felt like she was part of the conversation up front. The more animated Isabel and Maeve became, the quieter Katani felt. I could just as well not be here at all, she thought: for all anyone would even notice!

Boy, did Katani feel like the odd one out! Shouldn't Isabel

be the one feeling like an extra? She was the new one, right? And Katani was Maeve's best friend! So then why was Maeve acting like every single word that came out of Isabel's mouth was precious?

"Mom, Isabel's grandmother is from Mexico City. Isn't that totally cool? Remember that wonderful movie we saw last year about the Mexican artist? Well, Isabel's an artist, too," Maeve gushed on and on.

Katani hunched her shoulders over, the way she did when she was feeling tall and awkward.

Ms. Kaplan always seemed to know about fifty different people, whenever you said you were from someplace. When she heard Isabel was from Detroit she kept asking her, "Do you know so-and-so? ... Denise Cunningham," she said suddenly. "Do you know Denise Cunningham?"

Katani could never see the point of that. So what if Isabel did know one of these people? Then what? Would that make her any more special in Ms. Kaplan's eyes?

Stop it Katani, a voice inside her said harshly. You're just in a bad mood because you're jealous of her. You're jealous because she's new and pretty and everyone's so interested in her, and she's good at art, and so sure of herself ...

But Katani pushed the voice away.

"Here we are!" Maeve sang out as the car turned into a small cluster of stores lining Route 9.

And sure enough, they were there—at Fabric World, a place Katani usually adored with its rows of fabric. Even today, grim as her mood was, she couldn't help feeling her spirits lift a little as the three girls followed Ms. Kaplan into the brightly lit building and began looking at bolts and bolts of fabric. Maeve ran immediately to a row of glittery, sequined fabrics that would make much more sense for evening gowns than for blankets. "Omigod. I would so love a dress out of this for the first social dancing night. I swear to god, this stuff looks like something straight out of the Academy Awards!"

Katani almost smiled—but she stopped herself when she saw Isabel slip some of the gleaming silver fabric around her waist, trying it out. "How do I look, Maeve?"

Katani sighed, watching the two of them swoon together like they'd been best friends forever.

And I'm here because ...? she wondered to herself. This was getting worse by the minute.

Frustration was an understatement for how Katani was feeling. *Maeve shouldn't have even bothered asking me to come,* she thought bitterly. *She doesn't even care what I think ...*

She struggled to fight back that feeling. She does want my advice, she reminded herself. And I'm the one who knows about sewing. Isabel may be good at cartoons, but that won't help her here. She wandered through the store to the section where she knew the fleece was kept. She found three or four choices of material that she knew would work really well for Maeve's blankets, and tried to catch her friend's attention so she could show her what she'd found.

But Maeve was too busy swooning over the silks and sequins.

"Maeve," Katani finally said, trying to hide her annoyance. "If you really want to do this project, let me show you stuff that will work."

Maeve let herself be dragged—reluctantly—away from the evening gown material. She looked at the different colors of fleece Katani had chosen.

"You really think this stuff is the best?" she asked uncertainly. "Couldn't we use something a little more ... I don't know, a little more full of character?" She picked up some brightly colored cotton nearby, her face brightening. "Now this stuff is really darling."

"It's going to be hard to make a blanket out of cotton gingham," Katani told her. "You'd have to quilt that material to make it work. Fleece is definitely the way to go. It'll be really simple. You can just cut it with pinking shears, and maybe decorate it a little."

Maeve's face fell. "I don't want it to be that simple. I want to sew the blankets," she wailed.

"But Maeve, you don't know how to sew yet," Katani said impatiently.

"Oooooh," Isabel said, coming up as if out of nowhere behind them, and fingering the cotton gingham. "I love this, Maeve. Is this what you're going to use?"

"Whatever," Katani said shortly. "Go ahead, Maeve. Whatever you think." She folded her arms angrily across her chest.

If Maeve wanted to make really complicated blankets, let her. And if she got into trouble, let her new friend Isabel be the one to help. Frankly, Katani had had enough of the whole business!

THE CHANCE OF A LIFETIME

Charlotte's Journal
10 p.m.

> *I must've heard wrong.*
> *I was on my way downstairs from the Tower to get some graham crackers and peanut butter when I heard dad talking on the phone. For some weird reason I stopped to listen. And what I heard made me get goose bumps.*

You know that feeling when your heart almost stops beating?

Here's Dad: "I know. I know. It's the chance of a lifetime. They emailed me last week, and I finally got to talk with the head of the department today," he paused. "Right—Oxford. Can you imagine what it would be like to teach writing there? Even for just one term?" He paused again. "I know, Doug. I know." He was talking to Uncle Doug, about Oxford. My heart started pounding. I've traveled enough to know that Oxford is in England. England! A whole Atlantic Ocean away.

And we just got here!

"Right, I know," Dad said again. "It's just ... it's like a dream or something. When I think about walking on the very same streets that all those famous poets walked on ... John Donne, Samuel Johnson ... It's hard to believe that Professor Jones contacted me. That conference that we did together in Paris must've clinched it ..."

I crouched down, my mouth dry. It didn't take long to put two and two together. Dad has been offered a teaching job for the spring term in England. "Spring" meaning January. And England meaning back in Europe. It just can't be. After we just moved back here. After I've gotten all settled and finally found amazing friends and a school I love. Even with all the moves we've made, we have never, ever moved in the middle of a school year. It's one of dad's golden rules. I just couldn't believe this was happening. It was the worst nightmare imaginable.

I felt paralyzed.

It just wasn't fair. And why was I the last to know? Dad always talks first to me about serious things. Why wasn't he talking to me instead of to Uncle Doug?

Dad came up to tuck me in half an hour later and I couldn't even look at him. I felt—betrayed. Like he'd let me down. Like he was lying to me, just trying to act regular. "Hey," he says, leaning over to give me a kiss. "Char? Is something wrong?"

Wrong? My father has never, ever lied to me. Or kept something important hidden from me. How could he ask if anything was wrong? Just my whole life going down the drain, that's all.

"No Dad," I said, tears leaking down onto my pillow. I couldn't say anything. I heard him, didn't I? "The chance of a lifetime." "Like a dream or something." If he didn't want to tell me about it, it must be because he didn't trust me enough.

It came over me like a flash. He didn't want to tell me because he knew I wouldn't want to move. He has seen how happy I am in Brookline. He must want this awfully badly, then.

How could I ask him not to go?

I never really wanted to admit this before, but dad and staying put just don't go together.

Everything we own is travel-sized. He doesn't even have a real clock—just a travel alarm.

I love traveling too, but I have a home now. My heart is breaking.

As soon as he was gone I grabbed Truffles the Pig, my favorite stuffed animal. Make a wish, I told myself. But it was too cloudy to find the stars. I was crying hard. If Mom were here ... if she were still alive, we'd be a real family. With a real home, and a place we could really belong to.

How can I face everyone tomorrow?

I can't tell them. I just can't.

For one thing, they're not going to want to be best friends with me if I'm out of here in a couple of months. What's the point???

And another thing. If I tell them, that'll make it seem real.

I'm crying all over this journal even while I'm writing. And Marty is whining like he knows something is really wrong ... and he's right!

I feel like everything that matters most in the whole world is vanishing on me. I just can't believe it. It's not fair. It just isn't.

To: Sophie
From: Charlotte
Subject: England!

Cher Sophie:
So mon amie, it looks like my dream has ended. Tonight I overheard my father talking about a new job offer. In England. You were so right when you promised me that life here would get better. What I never imagined was that it could get so much better ... and then it could all just disappear. Remember that poem that we liked so much last year by Rilke—"all of life is a leave-taking?" I can't do it again, mon amie. Not another leave-taking. E-mail back and send advice. All my love
—Char

CHAPTER 5

❦

TRY OR NOT

CHARLOTTE FELT like she spent the next several days in a blur. When she woke the next morning, she tried to convince herself that what she'd overheard the night before was only a bad dream. And for a moment, with the sun streaming through her balcony window and Marty panting for attention at the end of her bed, it all seemed too distant—and too awful—to be true. Maybe it wasn't.

Her father *did* seem reassuringly like his usual self at the breakfast table—filled with good humor and lots of questions about how things were at school, and when he was going to get to see Katani, Avery, and Maeve again.

But in her heart Charlotte knew that it hadn't been a dream. As if to bring the whole terrible reality down to earth, that afternoon when she came home from school, she found a big thick envelope from Oxford University sitting on the front hall table, where Miss Pierce usually left their mail. Charlotte poked unhappily at the envelope with one finger. *I could throw it out*, she thought quickly. *Nobody would ever have to know. Mail gets lost all the time.*

❀

But she knew it was pointless. There were always emails, faxes, and telephone calls. Too bad they weren't living in the 19th century. Then she could keep her dad from learning more about—what had he called it?—"the chance of a lifetime."

Now, in the age of instant communications, she didn't feel like she could do anything.

She couldn't tell her friends. She couldn't tell Ms. Rodriguez or any of her other teachers. They'd all lose interest in her the second they found out. The only creature she seemed able to confide in was Marty.

"I can't stand it," she sniffled softly into his fur, hugging him tightly to her. "Marty, do you realize ..." She lifted her tear-stained face. Marty cocked his head to one side. He really seemed to be listening. "If Dad and I move to England ... what does that mean for you?"

Marty almost seemed to understand. He gave a low whimper and snuggled next to her on her bed, and Charlotte clung to him like she would never let go.

❦

"OK, Char. Let's hear it," Maeve said brightly at lunch the next day, taking out her bright pink notebook and a new pen, festooned with a huge pink feather. "How's your tryout coming for *The Sentinel*?"

Charlotte looked down at the turkey sandwich she'd made that morning. It didn't look very appetizing, but then she hadn't felt like eating anything for the past three days. "Uh ... what do you mean?" she asked slowly, stalling for time.

Avery pretended to choke on today's submarine sandwich. "Whoa. Do my ears deceive me or does our friend Charlotte Ramsey actually not understand a question?" she guffawed.

"What she means," she continued, with famous Avery irony, "is how's your tryout coming? You know, the piece of writing that Ms. Rodriguez wants turned in next Friday?"

The girls were at their usual lunch table. Isabel was sitting next to Maeve—the spot she'd taken since Monday—and Katani and Avery were down at the other end. Charlotte swallowed, trying to think of what to say.

"Oh," she finally said, thinking. "I don't know. I'm not sure I'm going to try out after all."

Avery snorted again. "That's a good one, Char," she told her. "Very nice. So you just write the letter, get the rule changed, and then don't go for it! And that totally makes sense because you're only the best writer in seventh grade."

"The whole school!" Maeve shrieked. She stared at Charlotte with wounded eyes. "You can't be serious. Even I'm thinking of trying out! But if you're not going to, how could I ever hope to get on? But I'm not doing it without you! Why wouldn't you submit something, Charlotte?" She narrowed her green eyes suspiciously. "Are you—you're not sick or something, are you?" She jumped up and tried to stretch her hand across the table to check Charlotte's temperature.

"No. I'm not sick. I just ... uh ... I just ... kind of changed my mind, that's all," Charlotte said shortly.

Maeve's eyes got rounder and rounder. "Do you ... is it ... writer's block?" she gasped. "Charlotte, are you stuck for an idea? 'Cause I've got tons of 'em. I'm just not much good at the writing part. Which is why I was kind of hoping that you'd help me," she added breathlessly.

It turned out that Maeve wasn't the only one planning to try out. Isabel wanted to try out, too. She wanted to draw her own comic strip.

"I'm kind of thinking of doing some sports writing,"

Avery added with a shrug. "But my mom and dad think I need to do something else—let me see, how did my mom put it?—something that exercises my brain, in addition to my body."

"What about you, Katani?" Maeve chirped up. "You could be *The Sentinel's* Fashion Design editor!"

"I don't think so," Katani said, a little annoyed. "Anyway, I've got my hands full these days," she added, looking away.

If she'd meant that last remark as a jab, Maeve didn't get it. She was too focused on Charlotte.

"I just don't understand it," she wailed. "Of all the people who ought to be trying out, Charlotte Ramsey, you're like—you're ..." She shook her head, her red waves tumbling around her face. "I just don't get it," was all she could say.

Charlotte bit her lip. There was so much she wanted to tell her friends. Suppose I go ahead and try out, she thought miserably, and suppose I'm lucky enough to get accepted on the staff—and then what? Tell them all that I can't really be on the paper, after all, because my dad's planning on moving to England?

"Look," she said suddenly, her eyes brimming with tears, "I just thought it over and it doesn't make sense for me to try out right now. OK?" And before one of her friends could object, she jumped up and fled from the cafeteria. She could hear Maeve calling her name but she didn't care. She just wanted to be alone.

Maeve:
Notes to Self

1. This newspaper thing ... I wonder if
   they need an advice column? Hmm—"Ask
   Maeve" sounds SO catchy. I could give
   people super good advice on all sorts
   of romance issues. I think *The
   Sentinel* needs something like that.
   Look how successful "Ask Beth" has
   been!

2. Find out what's up with Charlotte.
   I'm worried about her. Is she upset
   about Isabel?? Or is it something
   else? Maybe she's got writer's block
   and all her creative juices just dried
   up on her. I saw an old movie like
   that once and this poor woman with
   writer's block had to get put in an
   institution. I hope that doesn't
   happen to Charlotte.

3. Am I nuts or is Katani kind of mad at
   me??? I asked her if she could come
   over today to help Isabel and me make
   blankets and she came up with like 3
   different excuses why she couldn't.

4. Change I.M. away message: "If you're
   not living on the edge, you're taking
   up too much room."

5. Yuck—math test—HELP!!!

That afternoon, Maeve and Isabel knocked on Charlotte's door at about 4:30. Their arms were filled with shopping bags, each one stuffed to the brim with fabric.

"Charlotte! Help! We're working on blankets this afternoon and we decided we need the Tower room for inspiration," Maeve cried, sweeping past Charlotte before she could say a word.

Marty danced around Maeve's ankles, yelping excitedly. "Oooh," said Isabel, "this is such a cute dog." She bent down to pat him.

"Uh—" Charlotte frowned a little, looking from Isabel to Maeve. She wasn't in the mood for company today. What if her dad came home early and started talking about England again? What if they found out somehow?

"You know, I think I need a little time to think," she said quickly. "I'm trying to write, and ..."

But there was no stopping Maeve. "You should just see the Tower," she was gushing to Isabel. "It's the most magical place on earth. You're like up in the stars, and you can see all of Boston! It's the perfect place for inspiration. Which we kind of need," she added, racing up the stairs to the second floor.

Charlotte followed them, sighing. Long fingers of sunlight crossed through from the western windows. The old Victorian house always appealed to her the very most in the afternoons. As she followed her friends upstairs, she tried to imagine what it would feel like saying good-bye to this house. A lump formed in her throat.

Maeve was already showing Isabel around by the time she reached the Tower. Charlotte tried to see it through Isabel's eyes. It really was an incredibly wonderful room. Each window offered a spectacular view of the city from a different angle. Charlotte, Maeve, Katani, and Avery had decorated the Tower room and made it a magical getaway. Isabel's eyes sparkled as she looked around the room. She said that the Tower managed to feel mysterious and peaceful at the same time, though the serenity was shattered once Maeve had strewn her supplies all over the floor.

"Here we go," she sang out. "Cotton, scissors, quilting material ... what more could we possibly need?"

"So what's the plan, Maeve?" Isabel asked uncertainly, looking around at all the supplies.

"Here," Maeve said, fishing around in her book bag for a magazine. "I found the cutest picture of a blanket—isn't this sweet? And all we have to do is make more just like it."

Isabel looked a little confused. "That blanket looks kind of fancy, Maeve. How are we going to do all that quilting? And I'm not sure we can do that stuff—the embroidery. That looks pretty advanced."

"Have no fear!" Maeve sang out cheerfully. She took a pattern out of the bag, turned it over and over again, and then shrugged. "How hard can it be?" She opened the pattern and began taking one piece out at a time, scowling at the smaller ones. "I'm sure we don't need all of these," she said after a moment or two, wadding a few of them up. "Let's just—wing it!" And she began attacking a big piece of gingham material with some pinking shears.

If Charlotte hadn't been so anxious about her dad and the whole move to England, she would've started laughing when she saw the look on Maeve's face fifteen minutes later. There was cotton material everywhere—some pieces about the size of a handkerchief, cut ragged with Maeve's shears, and some much bigger. One piece looked more like a washcloth than a blanket. Maeve was concentrating furiously, cutting and cutting, but she was beginning to get stressed out. "This isn't working," she said finally, sitting back on her haunches. "I think we need to start sewing."

"But which parts do we sew? I don't get it," Isabel moaned.

"Darn, darn, darn. Where's Katani when we need her most?" Maeve muttered. She peered at the pattern's instructions again. "I think we need cotton filling. That's how it gets that nice thick quilted feeling. Oh dear," she sighed. "We haven't made much progress. I don't see how this is going to keep anybody very warm." She held up the washcloth-sized piece of cotton with a worried expression on her face.

"I think we need a break," Isabel agreed, pushing her dark hair back from her face. "Charlotte, can we go downstairs and get something cold to drink? All this cutting is making me kind of hot and sticky."

Charlotte laughed, and the three girls wound their way downstairs to the Ramseys' cheerful kitchen. Soon Charlotte was fixing glasses of cold juice for all three of them, and for the first time in days she'd almost forgotten the whole horrible mess with her father and his plans. It was so much fun to hang out with Maeve and Isabel. Marty was doing his usual leaping about for attention, so Charlotte picked him up and tucked him under her arm. That seemed to please him no end.

DISCOVERED!

Maeve climbed up onto the barstool near the telephone and began absentmindedly flipping through the pile of mail on the counter. "Hey, neat!" she exclaimed, pulling out a thick brochure. "Oxford! I love Oxford! I saw a wonderful old movie once about this glamorous guy who goes to university there and falls in love with a beautiful countess, only she won't talk to him because he isn't rich enough, and—" She stopped short, staring at Charlotte. "Hey, what's wrong?"

Charlotte could feel a rush of tears springing to her eyes. After all the tension of the last few days, it felt almost unbearable to watch Maeve thumbing through the brochure.

"Are you okay, Char?" Maeve demanded.

Charlotte struggled to regain her composure.

"What are you doing with a brochure from Oxford, anyway?" Maeve pressed her, as if she could almost tell something important was going on.

"I don't know," Charlotte stammered. "I just—"

Maeve had already begun inspecting it closely. "Hey, it's addressed to your dad," she said suddenly. She stared at Charlotte, her mind racing.

"Maeve, Isabel, promise not to say a word about this to anybody," Charlotte burst out.

"About what? I don't get it," Maeve continued, still staring at Charlotte.

Suddenly Charlotte couldn't keep it in any longer. "It's my dad," she burst out miserably. "I heard him the other night on the phone. He's been offered a job teaching at Oxford."

Maeve's mouth dropped open. She dropped the brochure as if it was burning hot, and the next minute had flung her arms around Charlotte. "Omigod!" she shrieked. "No wonder you've been acting so weird!"

"Thanks," Charlotte said dryly, trying to extricate herself from Maeve's exuberant hug.

"No, I just mean—it's so terrible," Maeve cried. "Isn't it obvious—you can't move to England! You just can't!"

Charlotte shook her head mournfully. "I didn't want you

guys to find out. It's hard enough having to worry about it myself, but I didn't want you guys to know. Promise you won't tell Katani and Avery," she added.

"This is terrible!" Maeve shrieked. "Charlotte, we have to do something!"

"I know," Charlotte said sadly. "The thing is, I can't think of anything."

"Does your dad know that you don't want to go?" Maeve asked, thinking hard.

Charlotte shook her head. "He doesn't even know that I know! I haven't said a word to him."

Maeve nodded. "OK," she said. "I think that's actually kind of good, Char."

"Why?"

"I don't know. But I think we need a plan. I'll tell you something, Charlotte Ramsey. We are not going to let you move all the way across the Atlantic!" She paused. "Not without a fight, anyway."

"I just don't see what we can do about it," Charlotte mumbled miserably.

"That's why we're going to have to tell Katani and Avery," Maeve said. Charlotte jumped up with a panicked look on her face. "I'm sorry," Maeve added "but this is a big problem, so we're all going to have to put our heads together to solve it!"

Charlotte's Journal
Wednesday night, 10:30

Maeve is a great friend. I don't know why it made me feel so much better now that she knows about Dad and England, but somehow it does. Tonight I actually felt like eating something really tasty ... and looking at the stars. I wanted to look at Sirius. That's Marty's constellation—the Dog Star. Too cloudy out to see much of anything, but at least I felt like looking again.

Now Maeve and Isabel know why I don't feel like trying out for The Sentinel. They both said they understood how I felt. I'm not positive Maeve completely got it, but I think Isabel saw my point—maybe because she's just been through a big move herself.

Maeve is positive that everything will be all right and that—together—we can somehow figure out some way to convince dad to stay in Boston. I hope she's right, but I don't know, I kind of doubt it. What can five seventh-grade girls do to change the mind of a grown-up? Sometimes I feel like grown-ups make things happen and we just have to fit in somehow. I know dad would hate it if he knew I felt this way. But it's hard to feel so powerless and small. I want to stay here so badly. My whole life is here now! It isn't just school, and my teachers, and the Beacon Street Girls—even though that's most of it. I love being back in Boston, close to where I was born and where mom and dad lived when I was a baby. This feels like home to me. I just have to make dad understand how important that is. But the question is, how?

And why hasn't he even told me about it yet?

To: Charlotte
From: Sophie
Subject: England!

Tant pis, mon amie. Your father is ... how
do we call it here? ... restless. He may
not even know why he has to keep moving.
No fair for you, my friend, to be uprooted
so soon. All I can send you is love and
good thoughts. All love, love, love
—Sophie

CHAPTER 6

⊗

THE SEVENTH-GRADE PAGE

HOMEROOM WAS noisier than usual on Friday morning. Pete Wexler was getting everyone charged up about Saturday afternoon's junior varsity game against Newton. Joline and Anna were whispering excitedly about some exclusive dance they'd heard might be happening at Brookline High School. Dillon was showing off the new cell phone he'd gotten the day before for his birthday. He was especially proud of the fact that he could customize the songs that played when the phone rang, and he had proceeded to show the class every single possibility. When Charlotte slid into her seat, Maeve was gushing over the phone—and Dillon.

"Oooh, I love that one," she said, leaning over his desk for a closer look.

Avery came bounding in, skateboard under one arm as usual. "Hey, guys!" she called out, leaping into her seat just before the bell rang. "Did I miss anything?"

"You missed my head by half an inch," Dillon complained, pretending to crouch in fear for his body. "Try

✿

to take it easy, Avery. This isn't a half-pipe, it's a classroom!"

Ms. Rodriguez came into the class, as if on cue. "Morning, everyone!" she called out with a smile.

Betsy's hand shot up. "Ms. Rodriguez? I'm wondering if you could update us about *The Sentinel* assignments," she said. "You never said exactly when they need to be turned in."

"Yeah," Dillon muttered, loud enough so everyone could hear. "Could you give us the hour, minute, and second, please, and make sure we know what time it's due in Japan and Europe, too, so we can put it in our Palm Pilots."

Maeve found that hysterical and laughed so hard she started coughing. Avery had to hit her on the back to get her to stop.

"OK, people. That's enough," Ms. Rodriguez said, shooting Dillon a frown. "I'm happy to go over this a bit today. After all, the deadline for the Seventh-Grade Page is only a week off, and some of you may want to talk a little bit about the best kind of samples to submit." She paused for a moment. "In fact, I think it might be a good idea to work on these for a while together in class."

Dillon groaned, giving Betsy a scowl. But Ms. Rodriguez was gaining enthusiasm. "OK, people. I want you to break into small groups and spend the next twenty minutes or so brainstorming. Even if you don't think you want to submit work to *The Sentinel*, I'd still like everyone to have the opportunity to try their hand at a piece of writing. So let's make this an assignment. Why don't you spend the next twenty minutes or so developing an idea for a story, feature, or piece of art that you'd like to submit to the paper?"

"Thanks a lot, Betsy," Dillon hissed. "Now you've gotten us an extra assignment. Another thing to write in that planner of yours."

Betsy ignored this. Her hand shot up again. "Would it be appropriate to write a feature about my test-prep class?" she asked.

Ms. Rodriguez cleared her throat. "Perhaps you might want to branch out a bit," she suggested mildly.

There was the usual racket as kids moved desks together to form groups. Charlotte and Avery were put together with Pete Wexler and Nick Montoya. Maeve got put with Dillon, Samantha Simmons, and Riley Lee—Charlotte could hear her burbling over with excitement as she dragged her desk in Dillon's direction. Katani was with Isabel and the Trentini twins on the other side of the room.

"Guess what I'm thinking of doing?" Charlotte could hear Maeve saying breathlessly to Dillon, as her desk bumped his. "An advice-for-the-lovelorn column!"

"A what?" Dillon asked.

"You know!" Maeve exclaimed, her bright eyes fixed on his. "Like suppose someone happens to really like someone else, and they don't really know how to tell them and everything. They write a letter to me, and I give them advice."

"Oh—cool," Dillon muttered, giving her a look like she was an alien who'd just crawled out of a spaceship.

Riley leaned way back in his desk, closing his eyes and yawning.

"How about you, Riley?" Maeve asked. "What are you planning on doing?"

"Dunno." Riley shrugged. Riley wasn't that big on using a lot of words. "Maybe some kind of alternative music thing," he mumbled.

"Great idea!" Maeve sang out. "You should do reviews, Riley. You could review new albums when they come out!"

Riley opened his eyes, looking faintly interested.

"Yeah—maybe," he said.

"Maybe I can review new gadgets," Dillon said, fingering his cell phone in his pocket.

Charlotte's group was making progress. Pete decided to write a sports column. Avery wanted to work on her Change a School Rule letter—the one about having to check off "other" in those little boxes they give you on school forms. Nick wanted to write a feature on rock-climbing—he'd been spending a lot of time out at Blue Hills in Milton, and was learning to use a harness. That left Charlotte.

"What are you thinking of doing?" Nick asked her, his brown eyes warm on hers. Nick had been friendly to Charlotte from the minute they met. He loved hearing about the adventures she'd shared with her dad, especially the stories from their times in Australia. Nick adored snorkeling and wanted to hear every last detail about the Great Barrier Reef. Lately, Charlotte had had the feeling that there was more than just friendship on Nick's part. He seemed to like her—a lot. And Charlotte ... well, she didn't know how she felt. Certainly not now.

"I don't know," Charlotte said slowly. Before the bombshell about her dad's potential job in England, she'd been thinking about trying to write an interview. But now, who knows? Charlotte's landlady, Miss Pierce, had a dear friend who was living in an assisted living residence in Brookline, and Charlotte had thought it would be really interesting to interview her, and to learn a little bit about what it was like to be ninety-three years old. Now, she was having a hard time mustering much enthusiasm for writing anything. Except maybe a letter to my dad, she thought sadly. A letter saying, "Please don't make us move—*again*."

Before she knew it, it was time to regroup and share their

plans with the class. Anna and Joline were planning to write a gossip column called "Wuz Up?" Samantha Simmons wanted to write a feature called "My Summer on the Cape." "It's really serene," she told the class. "It's so great to spend the summer on the beach, away from all the ... you know, the tensions of the city." She studied her perfectly manicured nails. "Of course, when you have your very own place, like we do, it's so much nicer than if you just have to rent. Or," — she looked a little horrified — "stay in a hotel."

Frantic eye rolling from Anna and Joline.

"Thanks, Samantha," Ms. Rodriguez murmured, one eyebrow raised.

Betsy had branched out to consider a "school calendar" page, filled with tips on how to stay organized.

"How about you, Isabel?" Ms. Rodriguez asked.

"I'm not sure," Isabel said slowly, giving Katani a quick glance. "But I'm kind of thinking of trying to do a cartoon."

"What a wonderful idea!" Ms. Rodriguez exclaimed. "*The Sentinel* hasn't had any cartoons that I know of. And I bet people would really enjoy that. What do the rest of you think?"

The class seemed to love Isabel's idea—a lot of people said something positive about it. Strangely, Charlotte noticed that Katani had a scowl on her face. *I wonder what's going on there?* Charlotte thought. Why wouldn't Katani like that idea? Katani was so artistic herself—it didn't really seem to make sense that she would not like a cartoon. Charlotte was beginning to really worry that Katani did not like Isabel at all.

But she was so preoccupied with her own worries about her father that she brushed aside her concern about Katani. She didn't even notice that Ms. Rodriguez didn't call on Katani or ask her what her plans were for the paper.

But Katani sure noticed.

All anyone cares about these days is Isabel. That girl opens her mouth and everyone thinks she's brilliant and fascinating, Katani steamed to herself.

Well, she wasn't planning on trying out for the paper in any case. She'd do the assignment for Ms. Rodriguez and be done with it. Let Isabel do her hot new cartoon and get all the attention! Katani was sick of her already—and Isabel had barely been at school for a week.

◌

A FRIEND IN NEED

"Katani!" Maeve was running, trying to catch up with Katani's long-legged strides. "Wait up!"

Katani was in a bad mood. "What's up?" she said, turning to Maeve without the slightest trace of a smile.

The girls were on their way to lunch, but first they had to stop at their lockers to dump their notebooks.

"Katani, listen. You know that pattern I chose for the blankets the other day?" Maeve twirled her locker with two quick spins. "Well, you were right. I think I may have kind of blown it a little. I mean, it's a really cute pattern and everything, but it looks a little too complicated for me. I tried to do some quilting, and I ended up sewing all the pieces to each other. Look!" She fished a wad of fabric out from her locker and held it up for Katani's inspection. It looked like a pincushion, with long tendrils of thread coming out from every angle.

Normally, Katani would have laughed her head off when she'd seen the results of Maeve's botched attempts at sewing. But she was still really upset about homeroom and being ignored by the whole class—and completely upstaged by Isabel. Again.

"I thought Isabel was helping," she said coldly.

Maeve was too high-spirited to pick up on Katani's wounded feelings.

"Well, she is, of course. She's such a sweetheart," she gushed.

"So why don't you ask Isabel to help, then?" Katani continued in a high, hurt voice.

"Well of course I'm planning on that! Only—"

"So great. So you don't need me," Katani said, slamming her locker shut. And before Maeve could say a single word, she had stormed off, leaving Maeve gaping after her.

Maeve:
Notes to Self

1. What is with Katani??? How can she be mad at me—what did I do wrong?
2. HELP HELP HELP these blankets are turning out to be a problem!
3. Idea for "Ask Maeve" column: Have a girl write in who really likes a guy (hint hint) but doesn't know how to ask him to get together (hint hint) and what should she do?

‰

Chat Room: BSG

File Edit People View Help

4 people here
- flikchic
- 4kicks
- Kgirl
- skywriter

flikchic: Hey guys we need to meet this aft we have an emergency!!
4kicks: what's going on
flikchic: we can't talk now have 2 meet
Kgirl: I'm supposed to walk Kelley home
4kicks: I have soccer practice
flikchic: what about 4:30 in the Tower
Kgirl: what's it about
flikchic: we have to talk later—this is 2 serious
4kicks: ok, I'll be there
skywriter: you guys are the best
flikchic: oh yeah I think Isabel should come 2
Kgirl: what's the deal with that?
flikchic: she's got good ideas and we could use them
4kicks: she's not a BSG is she lol
Kgirl: yeah did I miss something
flikchic: what's up with you guys??? She's really nice and she's new
skywriter: she might have some good ideas
Kgirl: g2g
4kicks: later guys
flikchic: where'd they go?
skywriter: dunno. I feel weird about the way they react to Isabel
flikchic: me 2

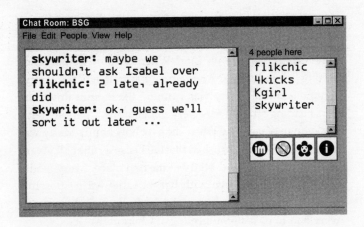

Chat Room: BSG

File Edit People View Help

skywriter: maybe we shouldn't ask Isabel over
flikchic: 2 late, already did
skywriter: ok, guess we'll sort it out later ...

4 people here

flikchic
4kicks
Kgirl
skywriter

INSIDE/OUTSIDE

Maeve was the first to arrive. "Geez, my mom is in the worst mood," she complained, sweeping past Charlotte into her front hall and crouching down to give Marty a kiss. "She is out of control. She says she wants me to start doubling up with my tutor—all because of one tiny little bad grade in math!" She dumped her overstuffed book bag in the hallway. "She didn't even want me coming over here today." Maeve looked pretty down. "And worst of all, she's threatening to have a big talk with my dad about my making blankets for homeless kids."

Even as preoccupied as she was with her own worries, Charlotte felt a wave of sympathy for Maeve. "Your blanket project is wonderful," she said warmly. "I'm sure your mom didn't really mean that you'd have to give it up."

Maeve sniffed. "She just wants me studying or taking lessons every single second of the day. I hate it," she muttered.

Before Charlotte could respond, the doorbell rang. Katani and Avery were on the doorstep. Neither looked all that thrilled to be there.

✿

"Hey," Avery said, coming in first and dropping her skateboard on top of Maeve's book bag. She looked from one to the other. "So, are we late? When does this emergency meeting get underway? And more important, where's Marty? Here he comes." Marty was running likety-split down the stairs heading straight for Avery's open arms. Charlotte felt a little twinge of jealousy when she saw how happy Marty was to see Avery. But she brushed it aside because, after all, Avery was the one who found Marty in the first place. Avery would love to have Marty live with her, but that wasn't possible because Avery's mom had really bad allergies. Marty and Avery had to be content meeting at Charlotte's.

Katani came in but didn't take off her jacket. She had her arms crossed, the way she always did when she was in a bad mood. "We can't be late for anything," she said pointedly. "Isabel isn't here yet."

"Hey, Katani, let up," Maeve said with a sigh. "This isn't the time for squabbling. Charlotte actually needs us!"

Katani rolled her eyes and didn't answer. Before anyone could say a word, the doorbell rang again. This time it was Isabel.

"Hi, guys!" she said, completely unaware of any tension in the room. "Charlotte, I just love this house," she went on. Then she caught sight of Marty, who was now scampering around Avery's feet.

"Ooo! Hi cute little guy!" she cried, bending down and grabbing Marty in her arms. She started giggling when he licked her face.

"Oh—be careful," Avery said suddenly, leaning over and scooping Marty back into her arms. "He can be kind of weird with people he doesn't know very well."

Isabel turned red. All the gladness seemed to go out of

her expression. Why were Avery and Katani making it so hard for Isabel? Didn't they have any idea how painful it could be to be new, trying to fit in?

It's as if they're bound and determined to shut Isabel out, she thought unhappily, leading her friends into the kitchen to make a plate of mini pizzas before heading up to the Tower. She hated that. It felt like she and Maeve were on one side, and Katani and Avery on the other. And stuck in the middle, with no idea of how the sides were being drawn, was Isabel. She had a sudden thought that this wasn't what the Beacon Street Girls were about.

CHAPTER 7

☙

MEETING IN THE TOWER

"OK, EVERYONE!" Maeve said, once they were all settled upstairs. "Here's the deal. Charlotte has a serious problem, and we have to figure out some way to help her."

The mood in the room changed—Charlotte had the sense that Katani was softening.

"What's the matter, Char?" Katani asked worriedly. "Is everything OK?"

Charlotte sighed. "Not really. The other day I overheard my dad talking on the phone, and it turns out that he's been offered a job to go teach at Oxford." When nobody said anything, she added, "Oxford—England."

"Whoa," Avery said. "England—that's awesome." Her eyes shone. "They have the most amazing soccer coaches there! Only they call it football," she added.

Maeve cleared her throat warningly. "Avery, England is on the other side of the Atlantic Ocean," she said pointedly.

"Oh—yeah, right," Avery said quickly. Her brown eyes fastened on Charlotte's as the implication of Oxford began to set in. "You don't think he's going to take it, do you? I mean, you just got here! We're all friends now."

"We've moved around a lot," Charlotte explained to Isabel, who looked a little bit left out. "My dad is a writer. My mom died when I was really little, and my dad ... I don't know, he loves to travel. We've been everywhere. We lived in Paris last year on a houseboat, and the year before that we were in Australia, and before that we were in Tanzania, and before that ..."

Isabel was amazed. "Wow. And I thought moving from Detroit to Boston was a big deal!"

"I love traveling," Charlotte said softly. "Just me and my dad. It was like the two of us on a nonstop adventure! I've loved getting to see different parts of the world and learning how other people do things. But now that I'm getting a little older, I feel different. I really want to settle down and have a home—at least for a while!" Her voice cracked a little. "I love you guys! I love Brookline and this house and the Tower and Marty ... I don't want to leave ... not ever!" Despite her best intentions, tears started to spill over.

Katani leaned over to give her a hug. "Oh, Charlotte," she said sadly. Then, with deep emotion, she blurted out, "I'll die if you have to move!"

Avery chewed her lip. "Huh," she said, thinking. "We've gotta get a plan, you guys. Charlotte, you can't let him do this to you. It's ..." She sat back, and came up with the absolute best word she could think of. "Unfair!"

"I know," Charlotte said unhappily. "But he's always dreamed of teaching at Oxford. It's got all this amazing history—all of his favorite writers and poets used to study there. I overheard him say that it was a job of a lifetime, a dream come true. And the thing about my dad is that when he has a dream, he usually makes it happen."

Isabel jumped to her feet, pacing back and forth a little. "I wonder," she said slowly, "if we couldn't figure out a way to make him change his mind."

Avery and Katani caught each other's eyes.

"What do you have in mind, Isabel?" Maeve asked eagerly.

"I don't know," Isabel said slowly. "I'm just thinking—if Charlotte's dad thinks he has his heart set on moving, maybe we should use a little reverse psychology to get him to change his mind."

"What do you mean?" Charlotte asked, confused.

"I'm not sure yet," Isabel murmured. "I'm just thinking ... sometimes my mom tries to get my older sister to do things that she doesn't want to do. Elena Maria is amazing at figuring out how to get her way by dropping little hints ... kind of letting her know what'll happen if she can't do what she wants to." She started giggling. "Like one time my sister got asked to a party with this guy she really liked, and my parents said she was too young to date. Well, Elena Maria pretended to go along with it. Instead of arguing with them, she just said, OK, fine. And then she said all this other stuff about how it was good that they were telling her how to handle this, because she probably wouldn't have the judgment to decide for herself. And that it was a good idea for them to make decisions for her. And how later, when she was older, she'd be able to ask them what to do whenever she was stuck.

"Next thing we knew, my parents disappeared for about an hour to have a 'discussion.'" Isabel grinned. "And they told Elena Maria that she could go after all! And that it was time for her to start making up her own mind, and making her own mistakes, because that was the only way she'd grow up to become a self-reliant adult!"

"Great story," Katani said, "but I don't really see how it

fits here, Isabel."

"Yeah—what's the connection?" Avery seconded.

"You guys!" Maeve wailed. "Don't be so negative! We need every bit of help we can get! And actually, I think Isabel's idea is kind of cool. Parents are usually backwards like that. In the movies 'reverse psychology' always seems to work!"

"So what am I supposed to do? Tell my dad how much I want to move to England?" Charlotte asked, confused.

"Maybe," Isabel said, shrugging. "Maybe if you point out all kinds of good things about moving that really aren't good at all, he'll realize how crazy it is to make you guys go."

"Couldn't it—I don't know, kind of backfire?" Charlotte worried. "What if I tell him how great it would be to move and he agrees?"

"Does anyone have any better ideas?" Maeve demanded.

The Tower room fell silent.

"OK, guess not," Maeve said. "So reverse psychology wins. Charlotte, for the next few days, you've got to be all over your dad. You've got to convince him of a million crummy reasons to uproot you and drag you back across the Atlantic!"

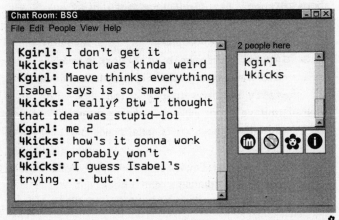

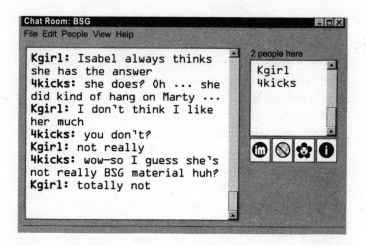

Chat Room: BSG

File Edit People View Help

Kgirl: Isabel always thinks she has the answer
4kicks: she does? Oh ... she did kind of hang on Marty ...
Kgirl: I don't think I like her much
4kicks: you don't?
Kgirl: not really
4kicks: wow—so I guess she's not really BSG material huh?
Kgirl: totally not

2 people here

Kgirl
4kicks

Maeve:
Notes to Self

1. These blankets need a little more work. Get Katani to help ... Why is K so mad?

2. Change I.M. away message: "Eating dinner. I'm single-handedly ridding the world of hunger—starting with myself."

3. Get Dillon to help with "Ask Maeve" column. Working closely together could really get the sparks going.

4. Shoe sale at Filene's Basement—ask Katani to go ... if she's not still mad!!!

5. Go to Party Favors for world's best chocolate cupcakes and check out all the new party toys. So fun!

Maeve and Isabel were upstairs in Maeve's bedroom on Saturday afternoon, looking with some dismay at the pile of cotton spread all over the room.

Isabel held up the fabric with a frown. "OK. It says we're supposed to sew piece A to piece B. That's simple. It's kind of like math," she said helpfully.

"I know!" Maeve wailed. "But I tried to do that, and look what I ended up with!" She held up a piece of gingham that looked something like a starfish. "This is not a blanket. Not even close. It couldn't even keep a spider warm!" They both giggled at the image.

A minute later the girls heard pounding on the door. In tumbled Sam, Maeve's super brainiac younger brother, who was dressed—as usual—in military fatigues. Sam was obsessed with military history. He had memorized every battle in every world war, and he had a collection of books that would rival the library at West Point Military Academy.

"What's up, weirdo?" Maeve said. "Can't you see Isabel and I are working here?"

Sam was tapping on the side of Maeve's guinea pigs' cage. "Hey, Lucy. Hey, Ricky," he called.

"They're not Lucy and Ricky anymore," Maeve told him, sighing heavily. "They're actually Lara and Zhivago now. Sam, I told you—we're working!"

"On what?" Sam asked curiously, picking up a scrap of fabric. "Hey—are you guys trying to make flags? This could be kind of cool for one of my battle scenes." He picked up a piece of cotton and pretended to wave it around, marching around the room.

"Sam," Maeve seethed, "could you do me a favor and march yourself downstairs and bug someone else? Isabel and

I are busy!"

Isabel giggled. "He's cute," she said, when Sam had left them alone.

"He's a total nerd ... and a weirdo," Maeve pronounced unsentimentally.

Isabel sighed. "I wish I had a brother. I always wanted one."

"Well, I'd kill for an older sister," Maeve told her. "I'd trade Sam in a heartbeat."

"Elena Maria's great," Isabel admitted. "But she can pull the big sister thing a lot. She always gets everything first. And my parents are completely fascinated by everything she does—she'll come home and tell a story about school, and they're all dazzled. By the time I tell something, it's all old news." She shrugged. "Anyway, it is what it is," she said with a smile.

Maeve looked at her admiringly. "You have the best outlook, Isabel. You're always so up about everything."

Isabel glanced down at the fabric she'd been holding. A shadow seemed to cross her face, and for just a moment she lost her sunny expression.

"Isabel? You OK?" Maeve asked, setting down her scissors.

Isabel hesitated for a second. "If I tell you something, do you promise not to tell anybody else? Even Charlotte?" she demanded.

"Sure," Maeve said, without thinking.

"It's about my mom," Isabel continued. She was still looking down, not meeting Maeve's gaze. "You know how I told you that we'd moved to Boston so she could have some tests done and stuff?"

Maeve nodded.

"Well, she's been seeing a new doctor at a hospital

downtown, and yesterday we got back some of the results. It's all still preliminary, but it looks she has multiple sclerosis."

"Multiple—what?" Maeve gasped. "Isabel, that sounds awful!"

Isabel had to smile. "It sounds scary," she admitted. "And it's kind of hard, learning what it is after waiting and wondering for so long. But they caught the disease in the early stage, they said, and her doctor thinks that if she gets treatment it may not get any worse. At least, not for a long time."

"So what is it?" Maeve wanted to know.

"It's like a disease of the nerves. It makes it hard for her muscles to work right. So she gets weak on one side, and sometimes she gets dizzy. She has to use a cane to walk right now, but the doctor thinks that should get better in a couple of months." Isabel sighed. "In some cases, if it doesn't get better, it could mean ending up in a wheelchair." Her eyes filled with tears. "That makes me so scared ... I'm just so used to seeing my mom being so strong. She's always worked and had time for Elena Maria and me, and time to run errands and do a zillion things. I'm just ... I don't know, it's hard to imagine her having to slow down. She's going to have to spend a lot of time at the doctor's while they figure out the best treatment for her. And she's going to need more and more help from my sister and me."

Maeve thought for a moment. "Well, she's lucky to have a daughter like you, Isabel. If anyone can help out, you're the one who can. You've got such a great outlook, and that'll help her the most. Just knowing that you believe she'll do great, and that she won't need a wheelchair—that will help a lot. But, if she does need a wheelchair, you shouldn't really be too scared about that. I mean, there are some really cool wheelchairs. You know ... the kind that go upstairs and spin around."

Isabel leaned over and gave Maeve a hug. "You know what? You're a great friend," she whispered. "It makes me feel so much better just telling you what's going on. I just really needed to share it with someone." She paused. "But remember, don't tell anyone else. Promise?"

Maeve thought of Avery and Katani, and she frowned. "Are you sure, Isabel? It might make ... I mean, it might just help, you know, if everyone else knew ..."

Isabel shook her head, her dark hair swinging. "No way. I don't want anyone feeling sorry for me or my mom. This is a family thing, Maeve. I really want to handle it on my own."

Maeve bit her lip. She had promised Isabel, and now she had to stick to her word. But she knew that if Katani and Avery knew what Isabel was going through, they would be nicer because they both were really good about things like that. But Maeve could tell that Isabel had somehow rubbed her friends the wrong way. And she wasn't feeling that hopeful that things were going to get better between them any time soon.

CR

Sunday night after dinner, Maeve's mother liked to take out the calendar and talk about "the week," as she put it.

Maeve tried hard to be patient with her mother, especially tonight. Hearing about Isabel's mom and what she was going through, she looked at her mother with new eyes. Imagine that her mom couldn't drive—if she couldn't hurry around the kitchen, the way she was right now, cleaning up and talking on the phone and doing what she called "multi-tasking." Maeve vowed, watching her mother just then, to work on getting along better with her. After all, her mother only wanted what was best for her—even if she didn't always go about it in the most tactful way.

"Maeve," her mother said, hanging up the cordless phone. "That was Ms. Teague." Ms. Teague was Maeve's tutor, whom she had seen once a week for as long as she could remember. "She's making space for you on Wednesdays and Saturday mornings from now on. That should help with math." She frowned. "At least I hope so."

"Mom!" Maeve wailed. "I don't want to go see Ms. Teague on Saturday mornings! I have a lot to do on the weekend! She is so boring! Plus I work so hard all week long, the last thing I want to do on Saturday mornings is study! Why can't you give me a break!"

"Maeve," her mother said crisply, crossing her arms. "We have been through this before. When you have learning issues, you have to work harder. You need to deal with schoolwork head on. You can't just pretend that things are going to get easier. We need to work at this, and I need your cooperation!"

Maeve's father wandered into the room, having overheard the last part of what her mother said. "What's going on?" he said mildly. Maeve's father was a big, hearty man with a round face and a beard. He tended to see the humor in situations that struck Maeve's mother as very serious. "Sounds like one of Sam's battle scenes raging here," he added.

"Dad," Maeve shrieked. "Mom is making me see Ms. Teague on Saturday mornings! That's not going to leave me time for anything."

"What do you have to do that's more important than studying?" her mother demanded.

"Carol," Maeve's father said, giving her mother a disapproving look.

"I'm serious, Ross! She needs to work harder or she's going to be in real trouble by eighth grade!" Maeve's mother burst out.

"I have lots of other things to do that matter to me." Maeve thought fast. She knew this wasn't a good time to bring up her friends—or Dillon—or shopping—or just having fun. "Like—what about my blanket project?" she sputtered.

"Good heavens. That project is getting totally out of hand," her mother shot back.

"It is not! I love my blanket project!"

"It's a mess," Sam interjected. "You should see it, Mom. She hasn't even made a single one. And they look like *flags*."

"Sam," Maeve's father said. "Don't get involved in this." He gave Maeve an affectionate smile. "I like your blankets, Maeve. I think it shows your heart's in the right place." He turned to Maeve's mother. "Carol, I'd like to talk about this later—alone."

"Don't start like that," Maeve's mother cried, getting angrier by the minute. "I happen to be the one who spends hours and hours organizing her schedule, I know what Maeve needs. And it isn't more time trying to make blankets, believe me!"

"Organizing her schedule and knowing what she needs aren't the same things," Maeve's father retorted.

The next thing Maeve knew, her parents were yelling at each other—and it wasn't about Maeve and the blankets anymore. They were both furious. "You never listen to what I'm saying!" "That's not what I'm trying to say!" "If you spent more time around here, maybe you'd understand!"

Sam gave Maeve a furious look. "Look what you've done," he shouted at her.

Maeve stuck her fingers in her ears. She couldn't stand it when her parents argued. The fact that this time it was her fault made it a million times worse.

> *Dear Maeve:*
>
> *I have a problim. I'm not always the worlds best student, and my mom realy wants me to be. I'd like to convinc her that I'm good at things—realy good. But some of those things have nothin to do with reading or writing or math. How can I get her to see I'm not a total messup?*

Answer:

Maeve bit the tip of her pencil. Outside, she could see the moon rising. Inside, there was just her laptop glowing at her. She had the question pretty well written. That part was easy ... except for the spelling, of course.

Now all she had to do was come up with the answer. How can you show someone you're not a total failure? She picked up one of her botched blankets with a sigh, her eyes filling with tears. Mom's right, she thought miserably. I'm rotten at math. And I'm rotten at making blankets, too. I'm not even any good at writing advice columns, since I don't have any advice to give. And I'm probably not even a good enough singer or dancer to go to Hollywood.

CHAPTER 8

REVERSE PSYCHOLOGY

OK, HERE GOES, Charlotte thought to herself, rinsing and putting away the last of the dinner dishes. Reverse psychology. She turned to her father, trying hard for a smile.

"Hey, Dad. How was your day?" she asked him, pulling a chair up to the table where her father was sitting with a stack of papers in front of him.

"Mmmm—pretty good," her father said, pushing his glasses up with one finger and giving her a smile. "Sorry to be so distracted, Charlotte. I just got in a huge batch of papers, and I'm trying my hardest to get a sense of this group. Some of them are excellent writers," he added, "but some of them need a bit of work, I fear."

"How do they seem, the American students?" Charlotte asked him. "I mean—compared to the students you taught last year in Paris? Do you miss teaching overseas?" There it goes, she thought. Is that reverse psychology? At least I'm leading into it.

Her father leaned back in his chair, looking thoughtful. "As a matter of fact, I do notice some big differences. And in lots of ways, I do miss living overseas. How about you, Charlotte? Are you missing Paris?"

Charlotte gulped. "Um ..." Now what? According to reverse psychology, wasn't she supposed to say yes? "Uh, sure," she said. "Europe is so cosmopolitan—and it has so many interesting people and cultures."

Her father glanced at her, surprised. "Really? I thought you were so happy here, Charlotte. As a matter of fact, there's something I've been wanting to talk to you about, but I was a little afraid to bring it up. I've been offered a job to teach writing at the University of Oxford. What do you think of that?"

Reverse psychology—reverse psychology, Charlotte thought wildly. "Oh—that sounds ... interesting," she blurted. Well, it was the reverse of how she felt, all right. She just hoped that Isabel really knew what she was talking about.

"Really?" her father looked amazed.

"Well—I mean—I think it's really important that you should get to do what you really want to do," Charlotte pushed on. There, that was better. "If you really want to teach in England, that's what matters. After all, I'm only twelve and a half. I can get used to anything."

Her father stared at her. "I hadn't really thought about it that way before. That's an interesting perspective, Charlotte." He pushed back his chair. "Let me show you the materials that they sent me. There's this wonderful new creative writing program that they're starting. And I'd be able to make up my own course!" He looked ecstatic, and Charlotte had to bite her lip not to burst into tears. She could never remember seeing her father this excited before.

For the next half hour, he showed her brochure after brochure. He even had a map of Oxford with little red dots

✿

that a realtor had faxed him. "These are some of the houses that we could rent," he told her. "They sound so charming, Charlotte. And there's a wonderful village school in a town called Abington where you could go. Although ..." He glanced at her, looking slightly uncomfortable. "I was worried that you've been through too many changes. The thought of uprooting you, especially in the middle of the school year ..."

Charlotte didn't know what to say. Maybe this was a good sign—maybe the reverse psychology was working.

"Oh," she said, trying for a breezy tone. "You know me, Dad. I'm so—adaptable."

"Yes," her father said slowly. Smiling, he turned back to the realtor's map. "You and I have always loved moving to new places together." He turned back to Charlotte with a wistful smile. "Remember when we first got to Paris? We couldn't get over the fact that we were going to be able to live on that houseboat together. It was like a dream."

Right, Charlotte thought miserably. Another dream. How could she explain to her father that she didn't want to live in a dream? She wanted things to be real. This was what she wanted—to stay right here in Brookline, with her friends, with Marty, with Miss Pierce. With her own little balcony and the beautiful view of the Boston skyline, and the Charles River and the stars.

So much for reverse psychology. She'd done what Isabel had suggested, and all that had happened was that she'd practically convinced her father to say yes to the new job. Charlotte made up some excuse to head upstairs, unable to watch her father enthusiastically studying the Oxford brochures for another minute.

It seemed like the Oxford move was as good as settled.

And Charlotte had mostly herself to blame ... and Isabel for helping to convince her father that it was the right idea.

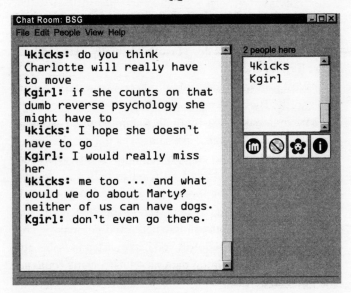

Chat Room: BSG

File Edit People View Help

4kicks: do you think Charlotte will really have to move
Kgirl: if she counts on that dumb reverse psychology she might have to
4kicks: I hope she doesn't have to go
Kgirl: I would really miss her
4kicks: me too ... and what would we do about Marty? neither of us can have dogs.
Kgirl: don't even go there.

2 people here

4kicks
Kgirl

UNRAVELING

Maeve took a deep breath, slinging her book bag over her shoulder. She spotted Katani halfway up the street heading to school, and she thought this was a good time to grab her friend and ask for help.

"Katani! Wait up!" she called.

Was it her imagination or did Katani look back over her shoulder and keep on walking?

But that was impossible. Maeve tried again, calling out a little louder this time. When Katani still didn't answer, she chased after her, out of breath by the time she'd caught up.

"Didn't you hear me calling you?" she gasped.

Katani didn't look all that excited to see her. "No," she said. She didn't quite meet Maeve's gaze. "What's up?" she asked, her voice sounding funny. Not at all like her usual self.

"Katani, listen. I have to ask you a huge favor. I'm kind of ... um ... I don't know how to put this exactly. But I'm kind of in over my head with this blanket thing. I really want to get it right." She took a deep breath. "Actually, I kind of have to get it right, and—"

"Why don't you ask Isabel to help you, then?" Katani said shortly. They had reached the front steps of school.

Maeve looked uneasily up at Katani. "I don't see what Isabel has to do with this," she said. "The thing is, Katani—"

But Katani had had enough. "I can *tell* you what she has to do with it," she retorted. "I tried to help you, Maeve. Remember when we were in Fabric World—which, incidentally, you dragged me to—and I tried to tell you that you should just get some simple fleece and not make such a major project out of this? And you had to listen to Isabel and get that ridiculous quilting pattern, which anyone could see was going to be a mess—"

"Katani! I'm sorry I just got excited about all the fabric ... you are not being very nice." Maeve was horrified and a little afraid. She'd never heard Katani this angry before—at least not with her. "I can't believe you could say that! And anyway, it wasn't Isabel's fault about that quilting pattern. I'm the one who thought it would work."

"There you go—defending her again," Katani shouted. "That's all you ever do. It makes me sick! That girl can do anything and you think it's perfect. Well, I can't stand it anymore. Fix your own dumb blankets!" Katani shrieked. And before Maeve could say another word, Katani had raced up the steps into the building, leaving Maeve gaping after her.

"I don't know what her problem is," Maeve fumed, stuffing her books into her locker.

"Whose problem?" Charlotte asked.

"Katani's. She just screamed at me," Maeve said miserably. "She was ranting and raving about Isabel. What's wrong with her? Why doesn't she like Isabel? And why's she so mad at me just because I do?"

Charlotte shook her head. "Katani doesn't like Isabel?" she repeated slowly. "Who could not like Isabel? She's great."

"Yeah, well, Katani obviously doesn't think so." Maeve slammed her locker shut, still fuming. "I'm pretty furious at her, to tell you the truth. And I don't care if she won't help me with my blankets. I'll figure it out myself—somehow."

Charlotte looked at her friend in dismay. Everything seemed like such a mess all of a sudden. Katani and Maeve were mad at each other. The "reverse psychology" plan that Isabel had suggested was backfiring—badly. It was hard to tell what might go wrong next.

CR

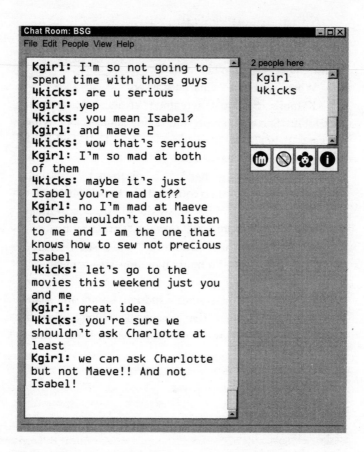

FIXED STARS

Charlotte let herself into the house and stooped down to give Marty a quick hug. "Hey," she said to him softly, smiling as she watched his tail wag like crazy. Suddenly, the door bell rang and Marty started barking like crazy. It was Avery.

"Hi Char. Thought I'd take the Marty man for a walk."

"That's great, because I have a lot of homework to do" Charlotte said.

As Avery and Marty raced off to the park Charlotte thought about how good Avery had been about keeping her promise to share responsibility for Marty when Miss Pierce said Marty could stay.

Sunlight was streaming through the big windows on the first floor; Charlotte loved this time of day. She headed upstairs, wandered into the kitchen and turned on the kettle to make hot chocolate, her favorite drink. It always helped her to concentrate. And she really wanted to work on her journalism assignment for Ms. Rodriguez.

But somehow, Charlotte just couldn't get inspired. Each idea that she thought of seemed wrong.

In the distance, she heard the front door turn. It was Miss Pierce, her landlady, who'd come back from doing some errands downtown.

"Maybe she'll have some ideas," Charlotte said to herself. She took her hot chocolate and wandered downstairs into the part of the house where Miss Pierce lived, knocking politely on her door.

"Why, hello Charlotte! What a nice surprise. Come in. I was just going to make myself a cup of tea," Miss Pierce said warmly.

Charlotte sank down on the soft couch that Miss Pierce kept in her kitchen. She looked admiringly around the room at Miss Pierce's "treasures" from a rich life filled with travels and work. Charlotte admired one of the beautiful framed photographs on the wall. "What's this?" she asked curiously.

"The double cluster," Miss Pierce told her, putting on her glasses for a better look. "It belongs to the constellation Perseus. It's really two clusters of stars, close together. Come have a look."

Charlotte looked closer. It always amazed her, these facts

about stars. What looked close was usually so far away. What looked like one was really two. Maybe that's why she loved stars so much—they made you question what you saw and what you believed in.

"Miss Pierce, can I ask you a question? What was it like—growing up here?" Charlotte asked her.

Miss Pierce tipped her head curiously at Charlotte. "It was very different back then," she said. "You know, I ran into some problems ... being half-Chinese in those days made for some strange comments from people. If it weren't for your friend's grandmother, Ruby, I would've been terribly lonely. But she and I had wonderful times together." She was quiet, musing back on the past. "Why? What makes you ask?"

Charlotte twirled her spoon in her mug of cocoa. "I don't know ... I've been thinking about it a lot. My dad—" she hesitated. "My dad is thinking of taking a job teaching in England in January. We might move again." Tears sprang to her eyes as she spoke.

Miss Pierce stared at her. "Oh, Charlotte," she said kindly. "Your father can't really want to move you in the middle of the year. You need to stay settled down for a while, child. Your father knows that! And if he doesn't ..." She looked earnestly at Charlotte. "If he doesn't, we'll just have to help him realize it."

"I think I made it all much worse," Charlotte said sadly. She filled Miss Pierce in on Isabel's "reverse psychology" plot. "So now my dad thinks that I think it's really OK to move. Even though it's the last thing I want!"

Miss Pierce sighed. "Oh, dear. Sometimes these plans don't really work, do they? Sometimes it's best just to be straightforward."

"I wish I'd tried that approach." Charlotte shook her

head. "I think I've learned my lesson on this one."

Then for the next hour, Charlotte and Miss Pierce talked about what it had been like for Miss Pierce as a girl growing up in Brookline—her friendship with Ruby Fields, the way they'd ridden the trolley into Boston together, and how much fun they'd had growing up together. They talked of the Tower and how the two girls, Ruby and Sapphire, had spent hours up there discussing their hopes and dreams for the future.

"It's extremely important to have a place that feels like home to you," Miss Pierce murmured. "Charlotte, perhaps you have to convey that to your father. Sometimes adults need to learn from children, and not just the other way around."

Charlotte got to her feet with a smile. "You know, you've given me an idea for the piece I need to write for school," she told Miss Pierce. Her eyes were shining. There was nothing Charlotte loved better than to challenge her imagination with a great writing idea. And she finally had the perfect subject to write about.

BELONGING

The Importance of a Place to Call Home

For many people, the idea of home is something to cherish. When people ask me where I grew up, I don't really know what to answer. The truth is that I have grown up in lots of places. Some of these I've loved. I loved the night sky over the Serengeti, where my father and I could find Orion—the one constellation I could find in both the northern and southern hemispheres. I loved our little houseboat on the Seine. I love knowing my way

✿

around airports and the way the sunrise looks when it shines through the clouds up at 36,000 feet.

But as I've grown older, I've come to realize that there is something missing in my life—a place filled with memories, rituals, and experiences. My biggest dream now is to be able to do something one year in the exact same way that I did the year before. Next year, I want to tiptoe downstairs and take out the Christmas tree ornaments and find them in the same spot where I know they are this year.

I have come to realize that there are many different reasons to travel. Travel can make you grow as a person. It can teach you many new things, like how you need to be very still in the bush if you want to see the cheetah hunt, or keep from stampeding a herd of zebras. Travel is full of adventure and wonderful surprises. But at a certain point, people need to build a place to which they can return. My biggest dream is that one day I will have a home like that.

I have always loved the constellation called the Seven Sisters. I've loved to think of those stars circling the skies together. If I could, I would make those seven sisters stop their traveling and stay still—long enough to let their light shine strong together. Long enough to know that for once, they're at home.

CHAPTER 9

❧

RULES TO LIVE BY

MAEVE HAD HAD a miserable day at school. Tuesdays were always hard days—she had the dreaded math quiz to worry about. And now how was she going to explain to her Hebrew School teacher that the blanket project couldn't possibly be ready for the presentation next month in her Bat Mitzvah class?

Dillon hadn't paid a single bit of attention to her in homeroom. Not even when she'd casually brandished the Social Dance Class invitation describing the first real night of dance class—a week from Wednesday. He'd just kept going on and on to Pete Wexler about the latest Patriots game.

Worst of all, Katani had totally snubbed her all day. Maeve had tried her hardest to smooth things over after their argument this morning, but Katani seemed like she didn't even want to talk to her. "She's giving me the silent treatment," Maeve told Charlotte. "I've tried three different times to get her to talk to me, but it's impossible."

The whole day had been horrible, and now she had only fifteen minutes before her mother picked her up. Usually Maeve hung out with Katani, Avery, and Charlotte after

✿

school on Tuesdays and Thursdays. But today that obviously wasn't going to happen. Katani and Avery had vanished the second the last bell rang. Charlotte was staying after school to talk to Ms. Rodriguez about something, and Isabel was walking home with her sister.

Maeve sat down on the front steps of the school. She was about to take out a notebook to start making some notes about her advice column when she caught sight of Ethel Weiss, the elderly woman who ran Irving's Toy and Card Shop two doors down from school.

Maeve had always loved Ethel. Her candy store was amazing—a tiny little store crammed with rows and rows of candy in every shape and size. She'd run the shop forever, or so it seemed to the kids who went to Abigail Adams. When Maeve was really little, back in second grade, she'd taken a Mounds bar from the store without paying. When Ethel found out, she didn't yell at Maeve or tell her parents. Instead, she asked Maeve to write her a letter about what she'd done, and why.

From that day on, Ethel was one of Maeve's personal heroes.

"You know," she said to herself, jumping to her feet. "I think I need to go see Ethel." Her mood brightened immediately. If anyone could give her some good advice today, it was Ethel. And some Necco Wafers or Swedish Fish would definitely improve her mood!

"OK," Ethel said a few minutes later, pulling a stool up near her cash register and offering for Maeve to sit down. "Tell me what the trouble is."

Maeve glanced at the faded piece of parchment on Ethel's wall displaying her famous "Code of Ethics"—a kind of guide on how to have a good life and good manners, too.

She smiled, feeling better already. Ethel would know what to do to make life right again.

"It's everything," she said. She told Ethel about her idea for the blanket project and how it had gotten out of hand. And how mad her mother was at her for not being able to focus and get something done right. "And now my mom and dad are arguing with each other about it, too." She shook her head unhappily. "But the worst thing is that Katani is angry with me because I asked Isabel for help and Katani's all furious and thinks that I should've asked her and now she isn't talking to me." Maeve took a deep breath. "So I've gotten everyone mad and my project's botched up."

"This sounds like trouble," Ethel agreed.

Maeve helped herself to one of Ethel's tissues and blew her nose. "I don't know what to do," she admitted. "I need to get Katani to stop being mad at me, I need to get Katani and Avery to realize how nice Isabel is and to quit avoiding her like the plague. And I need to do something about these blankets before I completely humiliate myself in front of my family and the whole of Brookline!"

Ethel pushed her glasses up on her nose. "This story reminds me of something," she said slowly. "You know, Maeve, you've done a pretty good job describing what needs to be done. Now all you have to do is make it happen!"

Maeve stared at her. "But how? I haven't the faintest idea how to make one of those things happen, let alone all of them."

Ethel smiled mysteriously. "Listen to yourself," she said gently. "And I think you really will see that you do know what to do."

She handed Maeve a bag of Swedish Fish candies, and Maeve helped herself. She didn't have the heart to tell Ethel that her advice had been less than helpful today.

Anyway, it was 3:30 already. Time to meet her mom and go to Hebrew School. Solving all of her crises was just going to have to wait.

ℭ

"Charlotte?" Mr. Ramsey knocked twice on her door. It was ten o'clock, and Charlotte had just slipped her journal under her pillow.

"Hey, Dad. Come on in," she called.

Marty was curled up at the end of her bed, his favorite sleeping spot. Mr. Ramsey gave him a little pat as he sat down on the edge of her bed. "I just got an email from the head of the English Department at Oxford," he told her, looking pretty excited. "He thinks there's a chance that the department could send us two tickets so we could go there at Thanksgiving and look around a little. You know — tour the department, have a look at the school that you'd be going to. Doesn't that sound like fun?"

Charlotte burrowed her head in her pillow. Thanksgiving? She'd been planning their first Thanksgiving in Boston already — what it would be like to cook a yummy turkey dinner in their cheerful kitchen — how excited Marty would be by the delicious aroma of good foods cooking in their oven. The last thing she wanted was to spend Thanksgiving in England.

"They don't even celebrate Thanksgiving over there, do they?" she croaked out.

Her father didn't seem to notice. "You know, I still can't get over your enthusiasm for this move, Charlotte. I was talking to one of my colleagues today at work, and she kept wondering how you felt about it. I told her that you were practically the one who's talking me into it!"

Charlotte squeezed her eyes shut tightly. Tell him, she thought miserably. Tell him that you don't want to go.

But he looked so unbelievably happy and excited, she couldn't bring herself to say a single word.

೧೩

NEW LUNCH TABLES

Charlotte and Maeve wound their way through the crowded cafeteria, both of them concentrating on balancing trays heavy with salad plates, juice, and the best thing the kitchen at Abigail Adams had to offer—giant chocolate chip cookies.

"That's funny," Maeve said, squinting a little. "Look—Katani and Avery are sitting at a different table."

Sure enough, Katani and Avery were sitting two tables away from our usual table—with Pete Wexler and another guy that Charlotte didn't know very well, Adam Jonas. There were two other open spaces beside them. Katani and Avery were leaning forward, talking animatedly to each other. If they noticed Maeve and Charlotte standing still and staring at them, they didn't show it.

"Oh no," Maeve said, frowning. "Isabel's all by herself over at our regular table. Now what?"

Charlotte glanced from one table to the next. "Uh ... can we ask Isabel to move over and join us with Katani and Avery?" she suggested. It didn't feel right to have lunch without Katani and Avery. They'd eaten together every single day since school had started.

"You ask," Maeve said, rocking back and forth from one foot to the other. "I'm not going to risk it. I think Katani's really mad at me."

"OK," Charlotte said slowly. "I will."

She walked over to Pete's table, still holding onto her tray. "Hi," she said. "Any chance we can join you?"

"Sure," Pete said, nodding at the two open spaces. Katani and Avery looked at Charlotte.

"Yeah, come on and join us," Avery exclaimed.

"Maeve's with me too," Charlotte continued. "And Isabel. She's all alone over there."

Katani and Avery glanced at each other.

"There's only two chairs here," Avery said, as if that wasn't obvious.

Charlotte felt a lump forming in her throat. Could this possibly be Avery and Katani—forcing her to choose like this? She couldn't believe her ears.

"It isn't fair to leave Isabel all by herself," Charlotte replied, trying to sound reasonable.

Avery shrugged, taking a big bite out of her tuna fish sandwich.

"OK," Charlotte said slowly. "I guess we'll eat over there, then. Like we always do," she added.

Katani looked at her briefly. "Nothing's 'like always' anymore," she said. Charlotte could tell how hurt she was by the sound of her voice, but she really didn't understand why. "If you guys are so big on Isabel, just go ahead and eat with her. It's up to you."

STUCK IN THE MIDDLE

"I feel so bad. I've put you guys in a terrible spot," Isabel whispered when Maeve and Charlotte joined her a minute later. Her beautiful eyes were dark and troubled. "I feel pretty awful about this whole thing. You should go ahead and sit with Katani and Avery, you guys. I know they don't like me. I'll be fine over here."

"Forget it," Maeve said. She took the dishes from her tray off one by one, setting them on the table with a flourish. Suddenly her face looked a little clearer, as if she'd decided something. "You know what, Isabel? If Katani and Avery want to be jerks for a little while, we'll just have to let them."

Charlotte looked uneasily back at her two dear friends, who were pretending not to look back over at their old lunch table. She wished she could feel as clear about all of this as Maeve did. It wasn't that she didn't like Isabel. She did! She just didn't want to lose Katani and Avery. The four of them were the Beacon Street Girls. Their friendship couldn't be over. It just couldn't.

DEADLINES!

Ms. Rodriguez was reminding the class that their journalism assignments would be due the day after tomorrow in homeroom.

"I've gotten to talk with several of you about what you're writing, and I'm really looking forward to being able to share these with the class," she told them. "I think we have a lot of great ideas coming out of this class. I have to tell you, I'm proud of everyone!"

"But we don't have to submit what we've written to the paper, do we?" Dillon asked anxiously.

"No," Ms. Rodriguez assured him. "Here's how it will work. Everyone will turn in what you've written on Friday. You still have a week to decide if you'd like your piece to be sent up to Jennifer at the editorial offices of *The Sentinel*. But don't be shy," she added. "Some of you are feeling a little more insecure than I think you should. You've got some great ideas to share, and I know the school would be that much richer for your contributions!"

Charlotte fiddled with her pencil. She knew for a fact that she wasn't going to submit her piece. For one thing, it was way too personal. And for another, she couldn't see the point of submitting something to the paper when it was already clear that she and her father were moving again.

It was hard to believe, looking around the room at the faces that had become so familiar to her, that by winter break she and her father would be packed and gone. No more adorable Marty to greet her when she came home from school. No more Miss Pierce. No more Beacon Street Girls. No more Abigail Adams Junior High. No more Tower room.

Charlotte bit her lip. She wasn't going to cry—not at school. And not at home, either. I'm getting good at hiding how I feel, she told herself, and it looks like I'm going to get lots of practice.

CHAPTER 10

❧

FAMILY FEUDS

WHEN MAEVE got home from Hebrew School that night, she was pretty upset. Everyone else in her Bat Mitzvah class had gotten up to give reports on their "mitzvahs," and it was clear that everyone else was ahead of Maeve. When it was her time to get up and describe what she was working on, she'd done her best to stall.

"I'm—um, it's still in the planning stages, really," she murmured, when Ms. Stein asked her to describe the blankets.

"Can you at least tell us what you're planning?" Ms. Stein had asked gently.

Planning—that was one of Maeve's favorite things. "Sure," she said, getting to her feet. "The plan is to have boxes and boxes of blankets to deliver to a homeless shelter in Boston. My dad has a friend who knows a wonderful shelter that really needs blankets for kids. He said he'd drive me down there with a few of my friends and we could pass the blankets out." Maeve was gaining enthusiasm as she described the scene—she could just picture it—passing out beautiful, warm blankets to homeless kids. Blankets made

❀

by kids for kids. She just knew the blankets would make a world of difference. "It isn't just about keeping warm on the outside," she explained to Ms. Stein and the rest of the class. "Blankets ... you know what it's like to have a special blanket to curl up with. It keeps you warm on the inside, too."

"Well, it sounds like a wonderful project," Ms. Stein told her.

Adele Jacobs, the star of the Hebrew class, gave Maeve a knowing look. "Sounds like it," she whispered to her best friend Katy. "But it also sounds kind of hard to pull off—if you know what I mean."

Maeve's face burned. Just because Adele and Katy always did everything perfectly—and on time—didn't mean they had to make her feel like a reject. It was bad enough knowing how much she had to do just to make the blanket project actually work. She didn't need them to cut her down.

Worst of all, she had confided in her mother on the way home.

"I just don't think I can make it happen, Mom!" she cried, jabbing the radio off as she slid into the front seat. "It's just too much. I've got so much homework at school, and all these activities—hip-hop and drama and Hebrew—and I'm never going to get the blankets together! I feel like a total failure," she said miserably.

The most difficult thing for Maeve was that her mother could be so sympathetic one minute and so angry the next. When she was sympathizing, Maeve found herself opening up and telling her everything. But then her mother would get angry, and use everything Maeve had just told her against her. That's what happened this time. For the first ten minutes, driving home, her mother seemed all ears—she really wanted to know why Maeve was feeling so stressed out, and what she could do to help. But by the time they'd reached home, her mood was changing. Maeve could feel her mother's frustration growing.

"You know, Maeve, I think you really need to be more organized," she said as they pulled into the garage. She was glancing critically at the piles of papers sticking out of Maeve's book bag, half of them crumpled, and some of them falling out onto the floor of the car.

"I'm organized enough. I've got my own system," Maeve told her defensively.

Big mistake. Her mother's eyes flashed. "If you were organized, you wouldn't be in such a jam right now, Maeve. I've told you over and over again that you need to have a system. If you'd just listen to me—"

Maeve knew she should keep her temper, but her blood was boiling. She couldn't stand it when her mother told her what to do—especially in the tone of voice she was using right now. "I don't need to listen to you!" she snapped. "I am not three years old, OK? What I need is a little more support—and a little more confidence from you that I can actually accomplish something ... OK!"

"How can I have confidence that you can accomplish this when you've just been telling me that it's all a mess and you can't possibly do it?" her mother demanded. They were halfway into the kitchen now, their voices rising.

"You treat me like an idiot!" Maeve cried. Tears sprang into her eyes. She couldn't stop herself now. "Just because I have dyslexia doesn't mean I'm retarded, OK?"

Her mother turned pale. "I never said that," she said, stunned.

"Said what?" Maeve's father came into the room, a frown on his face. He hated it when Maeve and her mother fought, which seemed to be happening more and more these days.

"She makes me feel like a moron," Maeve said, starting to cry. To make matters worse, Sam came running in to see what was going on.

"You're not a moron," Sam said worriedly.

He probably meant well, but Maeve wanted to smush him. "Shut up!" she yelled, throwing her book bag on the floor.

"Maeve, don't talk to your little brother that way," her mother said angrily.

"Carol, please don't shout," her father said, his own voice louder than usual just to make himself heard.

Soon all four of them were yelling. Maeve was accusing her parents of treating her like a three year old—even worse, a stupid three year old. Sam was yelling that he couldn't stand the yelling. Her father was shouting at everyone to stop it and her mother was on a rampage. "All over the place—disorganized—no sense of how to budget time—no sense of responsibility ..." She ranted and raved about all sorts of things that Maeve had done wrong over the past few months. Most of them seemed totally irrelevant. Her mother was clearly really mad, but she was crying, too.

"Carol! Please stop it right now!" Maeve's father said suddenly, with a new tone in his voice that made all four of them freeze.

Maeve's mother stared at him, her lip quivering. The next minute she'd walked out of the room, leaving the three of them in stunned silence. Of all the family fights they'd had lately, this one was the worst. And as usual, *it's my fault*, Maeve thought.

"Nice work, Maeve," Sam hissed at her before he ran off after their mother.

Maeve looked helplessly at her father. "I mess up

everything," she said brokenly.

Her father took her in his arms, stroking her hair. "Hey, sweetheart. Take it easy on yourself," he said gently. "You haven't messed up anything." He sighed. "I think ... I don't know. I just think we all need to calm down around here." He was staring out the window and he had a funny look on his face. It didn't make Maeve feel better, even with his arms around her. She felt like something was seriously wrong in her family. And she was certain that it was mostly because of her.

PASS THE PARSLEY ...

Charlotte took Marty's leash off and hung it on the coat rack. The little guy did his usual race-around-the-house trick at warp speed before he skidded into the kitchen in hopes of landing a snack.

"Charlotte?" Charlotte's father was in the kitchen, stirring something on the stove. It smelled good, but Charlotte didn't have much of an appetite.

"Pull up a chair. Come keep me company, sweetheart," her father suggested. The two of them loved to cook together and usually had their best conversations in the kitchen. But Charlotte had the sense tonight wasn't going to be one of those times.

"So tell me," her father continued, looking at Charlotte. "How are things with your friends these days? Isn't it high time for one of those Beacon Street Girls sleepovers you used to have all the time?"

Charlotte sighed. She wanted so badly to have a real talk with her father—to tell him some of the things that were going on at school. How Katani and Avery were mad at Maeve. How hard it was to welcome Isabel and get to know her without hurting Katani. How hard *everything* seemed all of a sudden. But she and her dad hadn't talked in so long—she didn't know how to get started.

"Maybe," she murmured. She tried to imagine inviting everyone over, and for a minute it seemed like a perfect plan. If Katani and Avery and Maeve could only be together again—up in the Tower—they'd forget all about being mad, and it would be just like old times.

But what about Isabel? She'd feel so miserable if she were excluded. And if I did invite her, Katani would be really unhappy.

"I don't know," Charlotte corrected herself. "Things are a little complicated at school right now."

This was the perfect lead-in. In the old days her father would have been all over that. What do you mean? What's different? Can you tell me about it? Her father was never the kind of person to let something like that just kind of hang there.

But her dad didn't even seem to notice what she'd said. What was up with him these days?

"Pass the parsley," he said. That was it! Pass the parsley—when she'd just tried to confide in him!

"Dad, you know, you seem kind of different these days," Charlotte said suddenly.

"What do you mean?" he asked, tasting the sauce.

"Just what I said. You haven't been ..." Charlotte tried to think of the best way to put this. "I don't know. You haven't asked that much about school or anything. You seem kind of preoccupied."

Her father looked at her with surprise. "Charlotte, I just finished asking you about school and your friends! But you didn't seem to want to say very much. Don't blame me if you're not feeling like confiding in your old dad these days," he added.

He was obviously trying for a light tone, but it didn't work. Charlotte was close to tears. "Have you ever wondered what it feels like," she continued, "moving to a new place every single year? Starting school over every fall and never getting to keep the same friends?"

Her father stared at her. "I always thought we had fun together," he said. He looked like she'd just put a dagger through his heart.

"We did," Charlotte said miserably. "I mean—we used to. It's just—I'm growing up now, Dad, and I think—"

The telephone rang, and they both stared at it.

"Let it ring," her father said. And at the exact same second, Charlotte said, "I'll get it." She picked up the phone, half glad that they'd been interrupted. She hated this kind of friction with her dad. She hated it so much. Talking with other kids her age, Charlotte knew that it was natural for kids to get into disagreements with their parents. But when you only have one parent, it felt different. Charlotte felt like the world was falling apart when she and her father were upset with each other.

The phone call was for her father. It was her uncle. "No," Charlotte heard her father saying. "No, not yet." He moved a few steps away from her, putting more seasonings into the pot. "No, I know. They said that I could have a few more weeks." He glanced at Charlotte. "No, I really can't—not right now. I'll call you later."

Charlotte bit her lip miserably. "Was that about Oxford?" she asked him.

He nodded.

"Dad ..." Charlotte began.

"Charlotte, I don't think this is a good time to talk about this," Mr. Ramsey said. "We're both tired, and it's been a long day. Let's wait for another time."

Charlotte felt queasy. She could never, ever remember a time when her father had shut her down when she wanted to talk. It was hard enough for her as it was to try to tell him how she felt about the job in England.

"Fine!" she snapped. That was it. If her father didn't want to talk, she wasn't going to talk. She ran out of the room, her eyes blinded with tears, and threw herself onto her bed, grabbing her mother's faded old jean jacket and burrowing her face in the fabric. Charlotte felt like she'd never missed her mother more. If only she were still alive, they'd be a real family—with a real home, and a real sense of belonging. She couldn't remember ever feeling more upset, or more alone. Even a snuggle with Truffles and Marty couldn't lift her spirits.

COLD WARS

On Thursday, everyone was talking about the journalism assignments, which were due the next day.

"What do you think?" Isabel asked Maeve and Charlotte at lunch. She showed them a draft of the cartoon she'd drawn.

Friendship ... it's such a leap of faith.

"I love this!" Maeve exclaimed. "Isabel, you're an awesome cartoonist!"

Unfortunately, Katani chose just that moment to walk past with Avery. Charlotte could see the two of them give each other looks. Not surprisingly, they didn't stop at their table, but went over to join Pete again.

✿

"Looks like the cold war is continuing," Charlotte whispered.

Isabel looked unhappily from Charlotte to Maeve. "You know what, guys? I'm feeling worse and worse about this. I think I'm just going to finish up my lunch hour in the library. I have lots of stuff to catch up on, and I want to finish the book I'm reading." Before either of them could say a word, she'd jumped to her feet and hurried off, dropping the rest of her lunch in the trash.

"That's it. I've had it. I am so mad," Maeve fumed. She jumped to her feet and marched over to Katani and Avery, who were just setting down their lunch trays. "Did you guys mean to be so rude? Or is it just starting to come naturally to both of you?" she demanded.

"What are you talking about?" Avery said, surprised. "Geez, Maeve. Could you just try to be a little rational for once?"

"Rational?" Maeve echoed. "Are you two nuts? Do you realize that you've been totally excluding Isabel every time you see her? And excuse me for being 'unrational,'" she added acidly, "but I don't think she's done a single thing to you."

"Irrational," Katani corrected her. "Not 'unrational.'"

"Katani Summers," Maeve cried, tears coming to her eyes, "you are so horrible."

Katani bit her lip. "I didn't mean that," she began.

But it was too late. Maeve was on a rampage. "You're mean to me. And you're really mean to Isabel. You don't know anything about her. You don't know what it's like to move to a new place where you don't know a soul. And she has problems too; you think you're the only one with problems! Well, you're not!"

"I'm sick of hearing about Isabel. She's so talented. She's

so good at art. She's just so—perfect," Katani snapped.

"Why do you have to be so mean about her? What is your problem?" Maeve demanded.

She and Katani were really raising their voices now, and several people were beginning to stare at them.

"Fight! Fight!" Dillon started chanting, with mock excitement.

"Dillon, don't be a jerk," Katani said.

This hardly made Maeve feel better. "He isn't a jerk," she said angrily.

"I can't believe you, Maeve. You've completely changed," Avery said, taking Katani's side. "You should just hear yourself. You're not even loyal to the Beacon Street Girls anymore!"

"Talk about loyal," Maeve snapped. She spun around to face Katani. "You promised to help me with my blankets. And then you—" She flung her arms dramatically. "You abandoned me!"

"I didn't abandon you," Katani retorted. "It's just that I obviously can't compete with Princess Isabel, that's all." She put on a mimicking tone. "Ooh, Isabel, you're so awesome!"

"Don't you think you both are being kind of childish?" Charlotte piped in. "Come on, Katani. There's room enough for two people to be good at things here, isn't there? And Maeve ... you did ask Katani to help you—and then you ignored her."

"Childish? Me?" Now Katani was really mad. "You know what? Avery is right about the Beacon Street Girls. We made real promises to each other. Only, clearly they weren't for keeps. At least, not for some people!"

"Who broke any promises?" Charlotte asked helplessly.

"Forget it. Let's get out of here, Avery," Katani said. She grabbed Avery by the arm. "And forget about the Beacon

Street Girls, too. Since you two obviously already have," she added.

Charlotte and Maeve stared after them.

"I don't believe it," Maeve whispered. "Char, what's happening? Everything is such a mess!"

"I know," Charlotte said sadly. She was barely talking to her father. It looked like within a matter of months, she wouldn't be living here anymore. And just now, when she needed her friends more than ever before, they'd all blown up at each other.

One bad thing had happened after another. It was time for *something* to go right. But it sure didn't feel like that was going to happen any time soon.

PART TWO

GOOD NEWS

୧୨

CHAPTER 11

ભ

THE HOMEROOM PAGE

"PEOPLE," Ms. Rodriguez said, after clearing her throat for the third time in a vain attempt to get everyone's attention. "People, take your seats now. I'd like to share some of the work you've turned in for our journalism unit." She flipped with interest through the stack of projects on her desk. "These are terrific," she added, looking up at the class with a smile. "You should all be proud of the effort you've put into this assignment."

"I liked this project," Betsy announced. "I was talking about it with my older brother—you know, the one who goes to Harvard?" She looked around, waiting for a reaction, but nobody seemed very impressed. "And he says that learning to work under deadline is really important."

"I think that's a good point," Ms. Rodriguez said mildly. She picked out one of the folders on top of her desk. "Avery, may I share this?"

Avery, who had been writing a note to herself on her notebook, sat up straight and nodded.

Ms. Rodriguez began to read from the folder.

✿

"I am a Korean-born American citizen with two parents who are Caucasian," she read out loud. *"I came to the United States when I was four months old. Ever since then, I've been living in Brookline with my mom and my two older brothers. There are a lot of things that matter to me—sports, for instance. Soccer, to be specific, and skateboarding too. I am also very interested in animal rights and speaking up for what you believe in. There are a number of things that make me the person I am. So, what I don't understand is why every time I take a standardized test, the first thing I have to do is tell the test makers who I am by checking off a little box. What is my race? This has really made me wonder—what is race, anyway? Am I 'Asian-American'? Is that who I am? My mom tells me I should just check off that box, but it doesn't feel right to me. I don't like the box that says 'other,' either. I am sick of being an 'other'!*

"For the past few weeks, I've been reading up on this subject. It turns out that lots of other people have the same problems I do. The U.S. Census asks every person living in the United States to fill out the same little boxes. If you're more than one thing, you're stuck having to say 'other.' Some people think there should be a new choice, which is to check all of the boxes that apply. I like that option. I want to be more than one thing, because that's who I really am!"

"This," Ms. Rodriguez told the class with a smile, "is an excellent example of an intelligent and heartfelt op-ed feature. An editorial. Avery has voiced her opinion loud and clear. Nice work!"

Everyone clapped, and Avery rotated her Red Sox cap around so that the brim half-covered her face. She always did that when she was embarrassed.

Ms. Rodriguez picked another one of the projects out of the pile, glancing it over quickly. "This is from Riley Lee. It's a review of a new music group, called the ..." She hesitated for a moment. "Am I reading this right? Is the group called xyz?"

Riley nodded. He was slumped in his chair in his usual "why am I here?" position. But he didn't look bored, for once.

"Can I share this with the class, Riley?" Ms. Rodriguez asked.

Riled shrugged. "Whatever," he mumbled. But he sat forward a little bit as she read his review out loud.

"*Xyz is a new, local band with a very cool sound. The drummer, Axton Cross, is a tight percussionist mixing several traditions. Dan Rivers is hot on the sax and the bass player, Ramone Tiero, has learned from the masters. This group plays eclectic jazz and is totally cool. If they can keep experimenting without losing their edge, this may be the best new jazz/rock band to come out of Boston in years. Their CD,* Random, *is available on their website—see details below.*"

The class loved Riley's review. Dillon whistled and stamped, before Ms. Rodriguez made him be quiet. Nick thumped Riley on the back. "Nice work!" he told him.

Riley looked embarrassed and proud at the same time. Charlotte realized that it was the first time she'd seen Riley look anything other than bored out of his mind all year.

"Riley, good job!" Ms. Rodriguez said, smiling at him. "Would you think about submitting this to *The Sentinel*?"

"I don't know. Maybe," Riley muttered, as everyone in the class started calling out encouragement.

"Riley! Riley!" Dillon cheered, again stamping his foot. Riley snuck a look at Maeve who was staring dreamily at Dillon.

"Dillon, please sit down," Ms. Rodriguez said, shaking her head. "If you guys can control yourselves, I'd like to share a few more of these." She closed her eyes and reached into the pile at random.

"Hmm," she said, scanning the page she'd withdrawn. "This one is called 'Wuz Up?—The Abigail Adams Gossip Sheet.' It's co-authored by Anna and Joline." She glanced across the room at the two girls, who erupted into giggles, as if the two of them were in on the biggest joke in history.

"Oooh—don't read it out loud," Anna begged, half-covering her face with her hands.

"Read it! Read it!" Dillon yelled, half-jumping out of his desk with excitement.

"Dillon, is there some reason you're repeating everything today?" Ms. Rodriguez asked mildly. She turned back to Anna and Joline with a quizzical expression. "If you are uncomfortable sharing this, I won't read it."

"Oh—go ahead," Joline said, ignoring Anna's pleas.

Ms. Rodriguez started to read out loud. "So just who is this certain ninth-grade hottie that has a new girl strutting her stuff? Do the initials G.H. do anything to anyone in this room who happens to have the initials I.M.? Oops, did we say I.M.?"

A couple of people giggled, a little uncertainly. Charlotte had no clue what Anna and Joline were talking about, but Isabel had turned bright red. G.H.? Who was that? Isabel couldn't possibly be interested in a ninth-grader—that was silly!

Katani coughed, as if trying to signal something to Avery. But Avery, who thought gossip was even sillier than shopping, was immersed in drawing a row of soccer balls on the front of her notebook.

Ms. Rodriguez cleared her throat. "Hmm," she said, scanning ahead. "I'm not sure if—"

"Come on, come on! You can't stop now!" a few kids pleaded.

Ms. Rodriguez continued reading, but she looked uneasy. "Who says that out-of-style clothes aren't making a comeback? Did we see a certain B.F. ..." Ms. Rodriguez stopped, frowning. "I don't think this one is made for sharing," she said firmly, setting the paper down and giving Anna and Joline a reproachful look. "I don't think a public forum like a newspaper is any place for comments that might be hurtful," she said disapprovingly. "I think I'd like to move on, if you don't mind."

Anna and Joline caught each other's eyes and gave each other one of their trademark expressions. Not for nothing, Charlotte thought, did Anna have that sticker on her locker that said, "It's an inside joke—and you're on the outside!" That was how she and Joline made everyone feel.

B.F.—wearing out-of-style clothes. Was that supposed to be Betsy? Fortunately, Betsy didn't seem to be paying much attention. She had her head deep in her planner, writing notes to herself. Ms. Rodriguez had saved her from embarrassment.

Maeve's piece was next. She hadn't turned in the letter that she'd written from the girl who was trying not to feel like a failure. She still didn't have an answer yet for that letter. But she'd written three separate letters to "Maeve," all from girls having trouble getting guys to pay attention to them. The last letter was her favorite. She tried to look knowingly in Dillon's direction as Ms. Rodriguez read the letter.

"Dear Maeve: My mom and dad have signed me up for Social Dance Class and I'm totally terrified that the guy I like won't even figure it out by then. How can I drop him some subtle hints so he knows to ask me to dance?" Signed, "Hoping to Dance With Him—Brookline, Mass."

The class looked riveted, including Dillon, though clearly he had no idea the letter had anything to do with him.

"Read the answer!" he called out. He gave Pete a nudge. "Listen up, guy. I think this could be kind of important for you," he told him.

Ms. Rodriguez smiled as she scanned the answer. "Dear Hoping, What kind of prehistoric era are you living in? Why don't you ask him to dance yourself? Chances are he likes you too, only he may not have the guts to show it. Once you get him out on the dance floor, the sparks will start flying!"

The class went crazy. Dillon started thumping Pete on the back, which Maeve found completely mystifying—did Dillon think she liked Pete? How thick could he be? Even Riley sat up and looked interested when everyone else started stamping and whistling.

"OK, I think we need to move on," Ms. Rodriguez said, holding up her hand. Turning in Maeve's direction she said, "Maeve, you captured the magazine advice format perfectly. Excellent job." No one had ever complimented Maeve on her writing before. She was stunned and almost felt like crying ... with joy this time.

For the rest of homeroom, everyone listened with fascination as they heard each other's work. There were book reviews, editorials, and even several pieces of investigative reporting. Abby Ross had interviewed two of the women who worked in the cafeteria. Avery and Pete's sports column was really well received, as was Katani's "Fashion Corner." And everyone loved Isabel's cartoon.

Charlotte knew she didn't have to worry about Ms. Rodriguez reading hers out loud. She'd written in red letters across the bottom of the page, *please don't share this*!! And she knew she could count on Ms. Rodriguez not to embarrass her.

Charlotte could barely read the piece she'd written herself without cringing. It seemed so corny now to think of writing about something like "belonging." Hah! *I don't belong anywhere,* she thought unhappily. *Not on The Sentinel. Not at Abigail Adams School. Not even up in the Tower anymore.* Normally Charlotte would have loved having the chance to listen to her friends and classmates' creativity. But not this morning. She was barely dragging herself through the motions—she didn't even really want to be here at all.

PRETTY AMAZING ...

"So—you're sure you can help me?" Maeve overheard Avery ask Katani. The two girls were standing together near their lockers, and Avery was writing a note to herself on her arm. "Call Katani! Help with website," she'd written in bright orange marker.

Maeve was just about to comment—usually, she'd say something like "Ugh, Avery, don't you think all those ink chemicals are going straight into your bloodstream through your pores?" But then she remembered: they weren't really talking to each other.

She opened her locker, making as much noise as possible, keeping her back to Katani and Avery and pretending like it made absolutely no difference to her whatsoever that her two best friends—ex best friends, she reminded herself grimly—were chattering away right behind her. She couldn't even share with them how excited Ms. Rodriguez's comments on her writing had made her feel. It gave her kind of an empty feeling inside.

Katani and Avery seemed to be hamming it up for her benefit. Since when were the two of them such major confidantes, anyway?

"I just can't believe he asked me," Avery said. She sneaked a look over at Maeve. "Can you?"

Who had asked Avery what? Maeve couldn't stand it. They knew how curious she was!

"I know," Katani went on. It felt like she was looking straight at Maeve the whole time she was talking. "I couldn't believe it either—when you told me. But you know, it really makes sense, Avery. You're a pretty amazing girl."

Maeve's face began to burn. They were torturing her. Who had asked Avery what? *Tell me!* She shrieked inwardly.

"But you know, this is all so new to me," Avery continued. "You really think I'll be able to handle this? You know my parents are totally, one hundred percent opposed to it. One hundred percent," she repeated earnestly—as if for Maeve's benefit.

"Don't worry, girlfriend," Katani said chummily, linking arms with Avery. "After school, OK? We'll go to work. And you won't be sorry you asked me for help." This last comment she said even more loudly than the rest, giving Maeve a superior look as she and Avery, arm-in-arm, hurried away together.

Right, Maeve thought angrily. I get the point, Katani. Like I should've let you help me, instead of blowing it and asking Isabel to help instead. I get what you're trying to say. Only I don't happen to agree!

Why couldn't more than one friend help? The blanket project had become enough of a mess for a whole army of friends to get involved! She moved away down the hallway, still dying to know what Avery and Katani had been talking about.

Suddenly, Maeve got it. Someone must have asked Avery to Social Dance Class! That must be it! What else could possibly have her wanting Katani's help? And she'd said she was new at all of this. And that her parents didn't like it! No doubt about it, Avery had snagged an invitation to the dance.

But from who?

"I can't believe he asked me," Avery had said.

"Me, either. But you're an amazing girl," Katani had told her.

Maeve's mouth felt dry. It couldn't be Dillon—it just couldn't be. However mad Avery was at Maeve, she wouldn't do that to her.

Maeve walked slowly toward the lunchroom, her heart pounding. It all made terrible sense. Avery and Pete had gotten pretty friendly lately—first, working together on their sports piece for the journalism assignment. Pete was good friends with Dillon. And—Maeve remembered with a sickening feeling in the pit of her stomach—for the past week now, Avery and Katani had been eating lunch with Dillon and Pete, every single day.

So that's what they're doing to get back at me, Maeve thought miserably. Avery's started flirting with Dillon, and now he's gone and asked her to the dance, and I'm ... I'm ...

She couldn't even finish her thought. She just wanted the floor to open up right then and there so she could crash right through it.

Avery didn't even want a boyfriend yet. And she hated dancing. Why would she go to the dance with Dillon— unless she just wanted to break Maeve's heart? This was getting worse and worse by the minute.

Just then Riley walked by. Head down, he mumbled a garbled "Hello." Maeve answered, if somewhat dispiritedly.

"Oh, hi Riley—nice review." That was the thing about Maeve. She always had a good word for everyone, even if she felt miserable herself.

THREE AGAINST TWO

"You guys seem awfully quiet today," Isabel said at lunchtime.

Quiet was an understatement. Maeve was slumped in her chair, watching morosely as Avery and Katani laughed themselves silly over at the next table with Dillon and Pete.

Charlotte didn't have much to say, either. She'd actually brought a book with her from the library and was tempted to start reading it—since Maeve didn't seem to feel like talking, and she didn't either.

Suddenly, Maeve sat up and gave Isabel a piercing look. "Hey," she said, "What was with that thing that Anna and Joline said today—about 'a new girl' crushing on some ninth grader named G.H.? Were they talking about you?"

Isabel blushed. This was the second time she'd reacted that way when "G.H." was mentioned, Maeve noticed.

"They're silly," she said lightly. "If they're talking about Gordie Hines, he's just a good friend of my sister's. That's all."

Maeve took a bite of her sandwich and put it back down again. "Yeah, well, silly is right when it comes to Anna and Joline." She sighed heavily. "But I'd still watch out if I were you, Isabel. You don't want them spreading gossip about you."

Isabel shrugged, with a "who cares?" look on her face. "Nobody believes that kind of garbage," she said, flipping back her hair. "Hey, Charlotte," she said, changing the subject. "How are things going with your dad? Have you tried the reverse psychology plan I told you about?"

Charlotte frowned. "Yeah—I tried it. It didn't work very

well," she said slowly.

"Really? Are you sure you did it right?" Isabel demanded.

Charlotte looked uncertain. Remember the Charlotte klutz-factor, she thought. It was entirely possible that she'd managed to botch this, too. "I thought I was doing it right. But it definitely backfired, Isabel. I started telling my dad all the reasons that it would be really great for him to think about taking the job—and how he shouldn't worry about me anyway. And the next thing I knew, he was agreeing with me!" Charlotte's lip started to wobble. "I feel like a number-one idiot. I think I talked my dad into taking the job!"

She could feel tears coming, and Charlotte hated having people see her cry. She jumped up and mumbled something about needing to go to the bathroom, leaving Isabel and Maeve staring after her. Here I go again, she thought miserably. Another botch-up from Charlotte the klutz. Trust me to take an ace plan and turn it into a disaster.

Isabel jumped to defend Charlotte. "Oh no. It's my fault, I never should've told her about the reverse psychology thing. It's just that it worked so well when Elena Maria did it!"

Maeve bit her lip. "Isabel, we've got to help Charlotte. This is terrible," she said quietly.

Everything else seemed to pale in comparison to this.

"What are you going to do?" Isabel demanded, watching as Maeve got to her feet, her face dark with determination.

"I don't know," Maeve said, marching over to the table where Katani and Avery were sitting. "But even if we're all mad at each other, I know that we have to help Charlotte. And we can't do it alone!"

CHAPTER 12

CR

BEACON STREET GIRLS
TO THE RESCUE

"OK—SAY something," Isabel whispered.

She and Maeve had walked boldly over to the next table where Katani and Avery were sitting with Dillon and Pete. But now that they were actually there, every word seemed to fly right out of Maeve's head.

"No—you," she whispered back.

"Forget it. I'm new!" Isabel hissed.

"Fine!" Maeve said. She marched up to the table and looked straight at Katani and Avery. Then her composure broke a little. "Uh ... hi," she said weakly.

Katani just looked at her. Avery twisted her Red Sox cap around, a sure sign that she was feeling fidgety.

"Can we talk to you guys?" Maeve blurted out.

"Ladies!" Dillon cried, with fake gallantry. He tried to pull a chair back for Maeve, but knocked it over instead, sending his drink crashing down at the same time. Some of it splattered across the table. Katani jumped up like it was poison, jerking back the edge of her sweater and shooting a look at Maeve.

As if everything is my fault these days, Maeve thought. Geez!

"Actually," Maeve said, taking the chair Dillon had offered her and trying to set it right, "uh, Dillon, Peter, we kind of need to talk to Avery and Katani ... alone."

"Girl talk," Isabel added hurriedly.

Dillon pretended to be hurt. "Please," he shrieked. "Don't worry about us! Don't worry that we're only halfway through lunch! Don't worry that there are no other seats free in this whole cafeteria!"

Maeve winced. She couldn't believe she was actually asking Dillon Johnson to leave. Here was the perfect opportunity to sit next to him and get in a good solid ten minutes of flirting time—and maybe give him the perfect opportunity to talk about Wednesday night.

Focus, Maeve, she warned herself. *Charlotte*. Charlotte is what is important here.

"I'm so sorry," she said. She actually did feel bad, and she didn't even try to sound flirtatious, which seemed to surprise Dillon. "You guys don't have to leave. Can we just kind of borrow Avery and Katani?"

Dillon gave her a funny look. "Hey. I was kidding," he said. He got up, really offering her his chair this time. "Take it, Maeve. Pete and I are going to go shoot some hoops anyway. Aren't we, Wexler?"

Maeve watched them leave. Dillon is actually a nice guy, she found herself thinking. Cute, yes—actually beyond cute. But also nice. She didn't know why that came as kind of a surprise.

"So," Avery said, from under the brim of her cap. "What's the big deal here? Why are you invading our lunch table? Where's Charlotte?"

"Charlotte," Maeve said dramatically, "is the problem."

"I happen to think there are several problems here," Katani said stiffly, sitting up in the straight way she did when she was really irritated. She gave Isabel a look.

"Katani," Maeve cried. "We're in a desperate mess and we can't possibly make it any better if we don't work together!"

"Mess? What mess?" Avery demanded.

"Well, you remember that Charlotte was going to try to get her dad not to take the job in England," Maeve began.

"I remember," Katani said. "Isabel had that great plan," she added, her voice filled with sarcasm. "What was it called again? 'Reverse' what?"

"Reverse psychology," Isabel said sorrowfully, hanging her head. "It backfired, Katani. Big time."

"Really?" Katani said, with feigned surprise.

"Katani, stop being so rude and help!" Maeve snapped.

Avery looked interested. "How did it backfire? I thought it was kind of a cool idea, actually." When Katani shot her a look, she added, "Well, it was."

Isabel shook her head. "It sounds like Charlotte's dad was just looking for an excuse to be excited about going. So every time Charlotte tried saying something kind of enthusiastic about the prospect of England, he jumped on it. Now he thinks she actually wants to move."

"Yikes," Avery said. "No Charlotte, no Marty, no Tower."

Katani was rolling a piece of paper between her fingers. "So, what are Avery and I supposed to do?" she asked slowly. "We're just kids, Maeve. We can't exactly change the mind of a grown-up."

Everyone was quiet for a minute. Maeve cleared her throat. "I don't see why not," she said finally. "You know— grown-ups don't have all the answers. I mean, Charlotte has been really happy here. What if her dad is making a big mistake? What if ... he's ..." she hesitated. "... running away from something. I don't know what, but I know it's wrong for him to be moving again when they just got here. Charlotte really needs our help, Katani."

"Yeah, Maeve, she probably does," Katani said slowly. She was still rolling and unrolling the piece of paper. "But you can't just mess stuff up and then expect other people to come in and fix it."

"Katani, lighten up a little," Avery admonished.

Maeve took a deep breath. "If you're talking about my blankets, forget it," she said quickly. "I'm over that. I don't care anymore. I only care about Charlotte."

"Fine," Katani snapped. "Fine. I'll help. I don't know how, but I'll help."

Maeve breathed a sigh of relief. Her eyes met Isabel's across the table, as if to say, *Phew. We're not dead yet.*

"OK. Let's meet at my house after school today. Just the four of us. Don't tell Charlotte—I don't want to make her feel any worse than she already does," Maeve said.

"Like this is ever going to work," Katani said to Avery, after Maeve and Isabel had gone.

Avery shrugged, taking out a red magic marker and writing "Maeve's house—4 pm" next to her social studies assignment on her left arm. "Well, it's worth a try," she said. "Though of course, you're talking to a girl who's still wearing her Red Sox cap!"

Katani laughed. Everyone knew that being loyal to the Boston Red Sox meant hoping against all odds—and never being defeatist. Maybe Avery was right. Maybe the only thing to do was to dive in and try to convince Mr. Ramsey to stay—however unlikely the prospects seemed of convincing him ... and however irritated she still felt when she thought about Maeve—and Isabel. After all, Charlotte was a best friend ... and a Beacon Street Girl.

BRAIN FOOD

Maeve hung her "Disturb Under Penalty of Death" sign on her bedroom door, and plopped down on the floor next to Isabel, Avery, and Katani. She'd brought a huge bowl of popcorn up from the kitchen and a pitcher of lemonade.

"Brain food," she said cheerfully, pushing the bowl in Katani's direction.

Katani was looking at something in the corner of the room. "What's that?" she asked.

Maeve looked, too. Following Katani's gaze, she saw the wadded up pile of cotton in the corner where she'd left it earlier that week. It was really just a heap of scraps on top of the untouched bolt of gingham, under Maeve's makeshift sign that read "Blanket Brookline With Love!" What was left of her blanket project, which at this stage wasn't much.

"Oh—nothing," Maeve said quickly.

Katani swallowed. She hadn't been up to Maeve's room for a long time. It was a lot harder being mad at Maeve now that she was actually here. Everywhere she looked, she saw something that reminded her of Maeve's amazing spirit. Her giant bulletin board completely covered with pictures—most of them of Charlotte, Avery, and Katani. Her movie star posters decorating the walls. Her stuffed animal collection, including her shaggy, oversized chicken, sitting right in the middle of her fluffy bed. Her two guinea pigs—this week Maeve was calling them Fred and Ginger—running around in their giant cage. And her beloved pink shag slippers, worn down to almost nothing, peeping out from under her bed.

Katani's eye fell on a piece of notepaper taped next to Maeve's bedside table. It wasn't in Maeve's writing. It was labeled "Schedule!" and it was a list of after-school activities, Monday through Saturday. Hip-hop dancing had been crossed off, and tutor had been added—in her mother's firm blue pen.

Katani felt funny. Looking around Maeve's small bedroom, it was really hard to remember what she'd been so furious about. Her eye fell on a new poster Maeve had pinned up. It was a picture of Orlando Bloom, looking mysterious and handsome somewhere on a set in New Zealand. "Note to self," Maeve had scrawled underneath the poster. "Orlando Bloom has dyslexia too!"

Katani suddenly felt ashamed. She shifted uncomfortably. "So ..." she murmured. "You really think we can do something to get Mr. Ramsey to change his mind?"

"I have an idea," Avery said suddenly. She'd been shooting rubber bands at Maeve's slippers, one by one, and she sat up, pulling off her cap. "Since the reverse psychology thing didn't work—"

"Sorry," Isabel interjected weakly, but Avery just shook her head.

"You never know with these plans," she said wisely. "But since it didn't work, what if we tried kind of an opposite tactic?"

"Like what?" Maeve demanded.

"Well, we kind of plant stuff. Secret stuff," Avery said, getting inspired. "Stuff that Mr. Ramsey will find that will convince him just how amazing and wonderful Brookline is. And Boston. We kind of work like secret, you know, public relations agents. Every good thing we can think of, we get into his head."

"What sort of stuff?" Isabel asked, looking interested.

"Maybe we start with a letter or something. We could describe everything that's wonderful about seventh grade at the Abigail Adams School. But the whole point would be to make it mysterious—Charlotte can't know about it. And her dad has to have no idea who's sending him the stuff, or planting it in the house. So he'll just keep getting sabotaged with all these mystery messages telling him why he has to stay."

"I like that," Maeve said slowly. "He's a writer, so he'll like that stuff."

"Maybe Miss Pierce," Katani added. "Since she's around all the time, she can put things in their apartment for us."

"Katani, that's great!" Maeve cried, her eyes shining.

Katani felt even worse. It was such a small suggestion, and Maeve seemed so grateful. I haven't been much of a friend lately, she thought unhappily. She couldn't remember now why she'd been so upset, or why she'd been so hurt that Maeve kept trying to include Isabel.

Isabel was just a girl—and a pretty nice one, too. Katani was beginning to feel like maybe she'd been the one with the problem, not Maeve.

IN FOCUS

The girls talked for the next hour, making lists and trying to divide up assignments. When they were out of lemonade, Katani offered to go down to the Kaplan-Taylors' kitchen to get some more. It's the least I can do, she thought.

She was halfway down the steps when she heard Maeve's mother on the phone.

"Liz, I'm telling you, I'm absolutely beside myself," she heard Maeve's mother say. "I think I already told you that we had to cut her hip-hop class so she can see Allie Teague another day each week. If we don't do that, I really don't see how she's going to pass math."

Katani froze. She knew she shouldn't be listening, but she didn't want to go back upstairs without more lemonade. And she couldn't go into the kitchen, either.

"I don't know!" Maeve's mother exclaimed. "It's not aptitude, believe me. She's got her father's intelligence—but she's also got his lack of focus. She's just all over the place. Liz, you should see this blanket project she's trying to do for Hebrew School. I'm so frustrated with it I could just tear my hair out. I've told her over and over again that she's not organized enough to do it—that it won't work. If she didn't have her father encouraging her ..."

Katani's heart started beating harder. Poor Maeve! She could barely imagine what it would be like to have dyslexia and worse, to have a mother constantly fussing about what you can't do, like Maeve's mom did. Katani's mother worked long hours as a lawyer, but she had always inspired all four of her daughters with a sense of confidence. Her motto was "There's nothing you can't do if you set your mind to it," and she believed that fiercely. She told Kelley that every day, though the words sometimes differed. That was one of the big reasons that Kelley was in public school, instead of in some special school for kids with severe learning problems. Katani's mom believed that if you raised the bar high, you could expect great things.

Imagine having your mother constantly on your back, criticizing you. It made Katani feel terrible. The more she listened to Maeve's mother telling her friend Liz that Maeve couldn't possibly get the blankets done in time—that she'd set herself up for certain failure—the more determined Katani became to show her that she was wrong.

❁

"Maeve's going to make those blankets, all right," Katani thought to herself, turning to go back upstairs. "And they're going to be absolutely fantastic, too."

Katani was bound and determined now to help Maeve with her project—even though—in fact, especially—because Maeve herself had stopped asking for any help at all. Katani knew that if they set their minds to it and worked as a team, they could do the project right.

It wasn't just about showing Ms. Kaplan, although the thought of proving Maeve's mother wrong definitely gave Katani a bit of pleasure. The important thing was to prove to Maeve that she could do it. She felt a wave of compassion for Maeve as she thought about how hard school must be for someone with a learning problem.

"Hey," Maeve said a minute later, when Katani came back into the bedroom with what seemed to be a look of "we're going to do this or else" on her face. "Katani! What happened to the lemonade?"

Katani started to laugh. She'd completely forgotten about the lemonade, but there was no way she was going to forget about Maeve and her blankets. That was too important.

CHAPTER 13

ൈ

SOCIAL DANCING

Charlotte's Journal
Monday night

Hey. I haven't written for days ... feels so weird to be curled up here on my bed with Marty, thinking about the week ahead, and feeling ... just kind of numb. It's not like me, but I'm just on autopilot. I've got three new books out from the library and don't even feel like reading.

Marty seems to get it. He just keeps looking up at me with these big eyes, like he knows that I need company.

Didn't even really cross paths with dad today. He had a late meeting, and I said I had a bunch of homework. He and I have to sit down and talk ... But we're both still feeling strange about the argument we had last week.

Today Ms. Rodriguez passed out some information about clubs, which begin after winter holidays. She just wanted us to be "looking ahead." I kind of got tears in my eyes and pretended I had to go to the bathroom. I can't stand the thought of things starting up and my not being

*here. I just can't bear the thought of leaving and having
to start all over again.*

Maeve:
Notes to Self

1. First Dance Class Weds. night—figure
   out what to wear. Shoes??
2. Tell everyone at Hebrew School the
   bad news—blanket project is a flop.
3. Hide from mom.

Isabel:

*Sometimes you gotta stop being a chicken
and try being yourself.*

Katani:
Today's Horoscope

Virgo: Excellent day for new business of all kinds! You're on top of your game, girl, and you know it. Lucky numbers are 7 and 15. Lucky colors, red and purple. Be sure to follow your dreams!

Avery's Blog:

Name: Avery Madden
Status: A Kid
Who I Am: This is the big question. Not what am I, which is what everyone goes on and on about, just because I'm adopted and my parents are white and I'm Korean. So you could say I'm half and half. But I'd rather say that I'm lots of things. I'm a soccer player. I'm a skateboarder and as of last winter, a snowboarder. I like poker and made-up card games (Click Here for more). I love animals of every kind. I share an adopted mutt named Marty with my friends.

Best books: The Lord of the Rings Best baseball team: The Red Sox

Random quote of the day: "I used to have a handle on life, but it broke."

BUÑUELOS

Tuesday afternoon, Charlotte walked home the usual way. She slowed down a little as she went past Montoya's Bakery, wondering whether she should go in for one of their famous iced hot chocolates. She wasn't really in the mood, but she felt like she could use a little cheering up.

Just as she was hesitating, Nick Montoya caught sight of her. He worked at his family's bakery after school several days a week, and today he was wiping down tables just inside the big window. He gave Charlotte a wave, motioning for her to come inside.

Well, she couldn't exactly just walk on by now without being rude.

Charlotte opened the door and went inside. A delicious aroma filled the air—cinnamon, chocolate—a totally heavenly combination.

"Mmmm. What smells so good?" she asked him.

"My sister's making a family recipe. It's a special treat from Colombia, called buñuelos," Nick told her. "It's kind of like a fried cookie, with cinnamon on it. They're really good," he added, grinning. "I had to help Fabiana out by sampling a few of them. You know, just to be sure that she got them right."

Charlotte followed Nick over to the counter, where trays of delicious-looking, S-shaped cookies were cooling down, sprinkled with cinnamon and sugar. "Have one," Nick urged her.

Before she knew it, Charlotte was sitting with Nick, tasting one of the cookies (she had to admit they were wonderful), and splitting an iced hot chocolate.

"Hey, when it's cold, this tastes so good with something sweet," Nick pointed out, drinking his half in one big gulp.

Charlotte nodded, but she didn't feel like joking around

with Nick the way she usually would.

"Are you OK? You seem kind of ... I don't know. Kind of quiet," Nick said, looking at her with concern.

"I'm—" For a second, Charlotte thought about telling Nick everything. About Isabel and the problems with her friends. About the move. About how she'd argued with her father and still felt really uncomfortable about it. Looking at Nick's warm, caring brown eyes, it seemed like the most natural thing in the world to confide in him.

"I'm just ... I don't know. I'm not feeling that great," she said in a rush. She knew he could tell by her expression that she wasn't telling him everything, but she couldn't help it. The words just seemed to leap out of her mouth.

"Oh," Nick said slowly. He started to concentrate very hard on his drink, stirring it with his teaspoon, tipping it back and forth a little. He wasn't looking at her at all. "Charlotte, I was kind of wondering ... you know how there's that dance class at the Community Center tomorrow night? Well ... I don't know ... Maybe if you're not feeling great you're not going to go," he said worriedly.

"Oh—that," Charlotte said, sitting up straighter. She'd forgotten all about the dance class. "No, I guess I'm going," she said. "Maeve would probably kill me if I didn't."

Nick looked down at the floor. "Some people are kind of ... asking other people to go with them," he said, as if it were just a point of information.

"I know." Charlotte thought about Maeve, who'd been hinting pretty blatantly to Dillon about just this thing.

"You think that's weird?" Nick asked, turning a little pink.

"I don't know—I mean, it's a class, not really a dance, right?" Charlotte said.

Nick nodded. "Yeah, you're right." He got to his feet,

still looking ill at ease. "But you are going? Right?"

"I'll definitely be there," Charlotte told him. She got up too, not really sure what to say.

Was Nick actually trying to ask her to go with him?

GETTING READY

Maeve was the one who had the idea for everyone to get ready together.

"Really?" Charlotte said. "Katani and Avery are coming, too?"

"Yep," Maeve said blithely. "We're meeting at my place, we're so near that we can all walk over together."

"But—are you sure Katani and Avery want to come?" Charlotte repeated.

"I am!" Maeve cried, twirling around and humming "I Feel Pretty" to herself. "Don't worry, don't worry," she added, seeing the puzzled look on Charlotte's face. "I know they were mad before, but things are ... I don't know, I think it's all better." She didn't want to tell Charlotte that they were all united again with a common goal: convincing Mr. Ramsey to stay in Boston. Not, she reminded herself, that they'd come up with a single idea yet. But they would.

"And Isabel?" Charlotte asked again.

"Charlotte Ramsey, stop worrying! Just show up at my house at 4 o'clock. And bring something really gorgeous to wear," Maeve instructed her. "Leave the rest up to me!"

OTHER DISASTERS

Isabel knocked on her mother's door. It was almost 4 o'clock, and she was supposed to be leaving for Maeve's house any minute.

"Mama?" she said. Her mother's bedroom was dark,

which meant she was resting. She was still getting used to the medication that Dr. Johnson had given her. It was going to help her a great deal in the long run, but for right now, it made her feel pretty crummy. It was hard for Isabel to get used to seeing her mom sleep so much during the day.

"It's just the pills—don't worry," her mother said now, sitting up a little bit in bed. "I called the doctor's office and he said he was pretty sure I'd be feeling much better by the end of the week."

"Good, Mama. I love you," Isabel said, sitting down on the side of the bed and leaning forward to stroke her mother's beautiful dark hair. Even when she wasn't feeling well, Isabel's mother was so beautiful. Isabel got a lump in her throat, remembering how she and Elena Maria had promised her father that they'd take care of her mother.

"Mama," she whispered. "Did you remember that tonight is the night I'm going with my new friends to the dance class?"

Her mother looked confused for a minute. "Oh—yes. I remember now. Will you tell Aunt Lourdes? She doesn't know, and she was expecting you for dinner." Her mother leaned back, looking tired. "I'm just going to rest a little bit now, OK? But come and tell me about the dance when you get home."

"I will, Mama," Isabel promised, giving her a kiss on the cheek.

She hurried out to the kitchen to grab her backpack. She'd already gotten all her clothes together—her favorite black miniskirt and a cute white top, and a pair of strappy black shoes she thought would be great for dancing in. Aunt Lourdes was busy at the stove, cooking dinner.

"Aunt Lourdes? Mama said to remind you that I'm going

out tonight," Isabel said, stuffing her makeup bag into the already-full backpack. "I should be home around nine, I think—"

Aunt Lourdes turned around, a quizzical look on her face. "Nine o'clock? It's a Wednesday night," she said slowly. "A school night."

"I know—but it's fine," Isabel said, not really focusing on her aunt's concern. "It's a dance class at the Community Center. All of the kids are going."

"Isabel, I don't like this." Aunt Lourdes crossed her arms, the dinner preparations forgotten. "Since when do you just take off in the dark and go out dancing? You're thirteen years old! And it's a school night," she added, as if that was the clincher.

"Mama knows about it," Isabel said calmly. "And she doesn't mind."

"Well, Mama's isn't the only vote around here!" Aunt Lourdes exploded. "This isn't Michigan, Isabel. Brookline is an urban area and it's just not OK for you to be running around at night—and I don't know who these kids are, and I don't know how you're getting there."

Isabel couldn't believe her ears. She and Elena Maria had grown up with pretty relaxed rules—their mother and father had always given them the benefit of the doubt, and trusted them to be responsible. Isabel knew that Aunt Lourdes was pretty strict—maybe not having any kids of her own was partly the reason for that. But she couldn't possibly have fathomed that Aunt Lourdes would try to override her mother's rules.

"Maybe you and Mama should talk about this," Isabel said, trying to stay calm. "But listen, Aunt Lourdes—my friends are expecting me. I have to go."

"I'd like you to ask me first!" her aunt said, looking angry and upset.

Just then the door burst open and Elena Maria came hurrying in. She had an armload of stuff, which she dumped in the hallway—her books, her soccer gear, and her bike helmet. "What's up?" she said cheerfully.

There was a tense silence in the room. Elena Maria glanced from her sister to her aunt. "Did I walk in on something?" she demanded.

"Actually—" Isabel and Aunt Lourdes said this at the same moment, then looked at each other and fell silent. If they hadn't been mad at each other, it would've been funny.

"Aunt Lourdes doesn't want me going to dance class at the Community Center. Even though Mama says it's fine," Isabel said unhappily.

"I just have a lot of questions about it!" her aunt exclaimed. "And I don't really appreciate finding out about stuff at the last minute, either! We're living together as a family now, and—"

"Please," a weak voice said from the hallway. It was their mother. She was in her bathrobe, and she had to hang onto the doorjamb to hold herself up. "I heard yelling. Can you please tell me what's going on here?"

Aunt Lourdes frowned. She was three years younger than Isabel's mother, and Isabel could see the change in her aunt the minute her mother came into the room. "I just didn't want Isabel running off in the night with strangers," she said quietly. "I don't think it's wise, I really don't—"

"Lourdes." Ms. Martinez shook her head, her face sad and weary. "It's hard enough being bedridden right now. I don't need to have you three quarreling." She turned to Isabel, who could see what a tremendous effort it took for her to move. "Isabel, go ahead. Have fun with your friends. We'll talk later."

Isabel glanced nervously from her aunt to her mother. "OK, Mama. I love you," she whispered. And with that, she was gone, sprinting down the hall of her aunt's apartment building to the elevator.

Living with Aunt Lourdes was proving to be a lot trickier than she'd imagined. Moving to a new place wasn't the hard part.

She missed her father terribly. She missed her mother being strong and well. And it was so difficult getting used to sharing their lives with their young aunt.

Isabel knew Aunt Lourdes meant well. But why did she always have to be so overprotective, and so incredibly strict?

CHANGING ...

"Isabel! Where were you? We were getting worried!" Maeve shrieked, pulling her friend into the house and dragging her upstairs. As usual, Maeve was in high-drama mode. "Did you bring something to change into?" she asked, looking worriedly at Isabel's blue jeans and navy sweater.

"Yep," Isabel said, starting to haul out her miniskirt and top. Thank heavens I had the good sense to hide this stuff, she thought, hauling out her makeup bag. If Aunt Lourdes had seen this ... She shuddered.

"I'm trying to decide between these earrings—and these," Maeve continued blithely, showing Isabel two pairs of enormous silver hoops. "Which do you like?"

Isabel laughed. "I think I like the silver hoops," she said.

Maeve's room was sheer chaos. Clothes, makeup, and accessories were strewn all over the place. Music was blaring from Maeve's pink stereo, which seemed to be setting off the guinea pigs, who were running around their cage and squeaking. Katani was in one corner making the final adjustments to her outfit, a stunning Katani number—silver miniskirt and a one-shoulder black top that looked fabulous on her statuesque figure.

"Katani! You look gorgeous!" Isabel breathed.

"Thanks," Katani said. She actually gave Isabel a smile—not much of a smile, but a smile just the same.

Charlotte and Avery were struggling to help each other in the other corner. Avery had her soccer clothes on and was scowling at a limp piece of fabric in her hand. "You can't really expect me to put this on," she mumbled. "I'll freeze to death in this thing!"

Charlotte was halfway into her favorite bohemian skirt from Paris, and she didn't look all that thrilled either.

"What do you guys think?" Maeve asked, leaping onto her bed so she could see herself in the mirror across the room. She tried to turn around and get a look at herself from behind, and almost fell off the bed.

"Oops!" she said, catching herself.

Maeve had really outdone herself tonight. She was wearing a bright blue dress with a trendy design that showed every curve in her very curvy figure. High strappy heels finished the look—along with her huge hoops.

"Blue is Dillon's favorite color," Maeve pointed out, squinting at herself.

"You really like Dillon, don't you?" Isabel asked.

Maeve tried to look nonchalant. "He's OK," she said. She glanced at Isabel. "What about you? I saw Pete looking at you in homeroom the other day ..."

Isabel shrugged. "Seventh-grade guys seem kind of

young to me," she said, leaning forward to buckle the strap on her high heel.

"How you expect to be able to move in those shoes is beyond me," Avery remarked.

"And what are you planning on wearing? Soccer cleats?" Maeve retorted.

"Not sure," Avery mumbled. "Can't I just wear sneakers? Aren't we learning to dance?"

"You can't wear sneakers!" Katani looked horrified.

"Kidding, Katani. Just kidding," Avery said. She pulled a pair of black flats out of her soccer bag. "My mom has spent half her life at Social Dancing. She's out of her mind about this. She thinks it will actually make me a 'young lady.' "

Maeve shook her head. "You make that sound like a fate worse than death," she chided her.

Avery jumped up on the bed. "My turn for the stage, Maeve. Here's a story called 'Averella,' starring Avery Madden and written by her mother:

"Once upon a time a girl named Averella was growing up in a house with her perfect mother and her two perfect brothers. And on vacations, she occasionally hung out with her father. Only Averella was always a mess. Messy hair, messy face, messy locker," she added ruefully. "Anyway, she got invited to a fabulous ball. Now when Averella heard the word 'ball,' all she could think of was soccer. But no. At this ball you were supposed to wear very uncomfortable shoes and wait for some guy to ask you to dance. Boring. Still, Averella went to the ball. And guess what? She turned into a regular lady. Soon she curled her hair and wanted to spend all her free time reading fashion magazines and going shopping."

"That's a happy ending?" Maeve asked, frowning. She was still irritated with Avery, whom she was convinced was trying to get Dillon to like her. Though she had to admit it didn't look like Avery was planning on using high fashion as bait!

"Not to me," Avery said, hopping down from the bed and trying to stuff one of her feet into a black flat.

"I have another ending," Katani said, tossing Avery a hairbrush. "Averella went to the dance. And she learned something new, and actually had a good time. And she still played soccer, and she realized that going to a dance did not completely destroy her credibility."

"Hmm," Avery said, looking at her thoughtfully. "Kind of like Check All That Apply," she added, half to herself. She wriggled into her dress, pulling up the zipper from behind.

That did it. All five of them were dressed.

"I think we need a group picture," Maeve exclaimed. "Let's go downstairs and get my mom."

Five minutes later, the five girls were lined up together in Maeve's kitchen, arms linked.

"Maeve, you have a tiny bit of lipstick on your tooth," Maeve's mother said.

Katani passed Maeve a tissue. It figures, she thought. Could Ms. Kaplan possibly say something to Maeve without being critical?

But Maeve was so excited she didn't seem to mind. "This is a perfect night," she announced. "Getting ready for the dance class—all five of us! Right, girls?"

Katani smiled at her. Maeve really did have her heart in the right place, she thought affectionately. True, she could be a little spacey sometimes. And she'd laid it on a little thick welcoming Isabel. But way down deep, Katani realized that Maeve was a pretty good person after all.

CHAPTER 14

❧

GIRLS' CHOICE

THE BROOKLINE Community Center had been transformed for the opening night of Social Dance Class. The big central room was darkened, big tables with refreshments set up on either side of the room, and a music system played welcoming music as seventh graders streamed into the building. There were several other Brookline junior highs participating as well, so the Beacon Street Girls saw many unfamiliar faces— as well as lots of kids they knew from school.

"OMG—the Queens of Mean, in dresses," Maeve hissed, grabbing Katani's arm.

Avery followed her gaze. "Oh—and look, there's Dillon," she said.

It was an innocent comment, but Maeve jumped on it. "I know. I see him," she cried, racing off to make sure she was the first to say Hi.

Avery frowned. "What gives? Is this place making everyone act like an alien?" She rubbed her arms. "I'm freezing, anyway. I want my sweatshirt," she moaned to Katani.

The four girls moved over toward the refreshment table

while Maeve cornered Dillon.

"Hey," she said, trying to lower her eyes just the way Audrey Hepburn does in Maeve's all-time favorite movie, *Sabrina*. "You look great, Dillon."

"Thanks," Dillon said. "Personally I hate this tie-and-jacket thing. I seriously feel like I'm being strangled." He looked more closely at Maeve. "Are you OK? Do you have something in your eye?"

Maeve gave up with her eyelowering act. Subtlety, she thought with a sigh, is just lost on seventh-grade guys.

"You know, Dillon," she said coyly. "After we learn a few dances, we're going to have free choice. And I was thinking—"

"Gotta go," Dillon said abruptly, catching sight of Pete Wexler, who was waving desperately at him across the room.

Maeve chewed her lip as she wandered back to find her friends.

"What's wrong, Maeve? Shoes hurting?" Avery asked with apparent sincerity, helping herself to some 7-Up.

Maeve gave her a suspicious look. "Avery," she said suddenly, leaning closer, "what do you think of Dillon?"

"He's OK," Avery said with a shrug. "Why?"

Maeve didn't answer—she was too busy fuming. For Avery to say a guy was OK ... well, that clinched it. While Avery and Katani had been mad at her, they'd been hanging out nonstop with Pete and Dillon. It was obvious that Avery had really fallen for Dillon ... Well, she wasn't going to just let Avery steal Dillon from her. No way. Tonight was the chance to prove once and for all that Dillon was hers. And Avery was just going to have to stay out of her way!

Jody Brown, the Social Dance teacher, got the formal part of the evening started about five minutes later. She was a petite brunette with a lot of energy. "She's young," Katani whispered to Maeve, surprised.

"Here's the agenda for tonight," Jody announced, clearly not at all perturbed by the fact that she had more than a hundred seventh graders milling around. "For an hour, we're going to work on the basics of ballroom dancing—the box step. We'll try it first without music, then with. Once you've got that down, I'll show you how you can put it to a beat and it becomes the Foxtrot. After that, we'll have some refreshments, and the last hour of the evening you can dance however you like."

"Foxtrot? That sounds like a soccer play," Avery muttered.

"Sshhhh," Maeve said, more sternly than normal.

Jody continued to lay out the ground rules. For the instruction part of class, kids would be matched up by pulling numbers out of two boxes on the refreshment table. "For free dancing, you guys can pick your own partners," she added. This of course prompted some serious hooting from the back of the room, but Jody didn't seem phased by it.

There was some confusion while everyone picked his or her numbers. Maeve tried to hide a groan when she discovered she was paired up with Riley Lee. Katani got a guy named Joe from another junior high school, and Charlotte got someone she didn't know very well—Sammy Andropovitch, a boy in her homeroom who was extremely shy. And short, she thought ruefully. Sammy barely made it up to her shoulders.

Isabel got paired with Billy Trentini. Unbelievably—in Maeve's mind, anyway—Avery got Dillon.

This has got to be rigged, she thought furiously, trying her best not to trip Avery as she bounded over toward Dillon, calling out his name. She couldn't see how Avery had pulled this one off, but she'd clearly managed something sneaky with this one.

"Watch it, Madden. That's my foot, not a soccer ball," Dillon cried, pretending to jump up and down in pain.

Flirting already, Maeve fumed.

"Come on, Maeve. We're supposed to stand and face each other," Riley told her.

Maeve sighed. "OK, OK." She followed Riley to their spot on the dance floor, trying hard not to think about having to hold his hand—and worse, having him hold her waist—for the next hour.

"I think we stand like this," Charlotte said gently to Sammy, trying to guide him into the position Jody and her partner Jim were demonstrating on the stage.

Sammy turned beet red. If he stood that way and faced her, he was staring directly into her chest!

Maeve fought the urge to wipe her hand on her dress. She could have guessed that Riley had slippery hands. Yuck!

Isabel was gently trying to dislodge Billy's foot, which seemed to keep landing on hers.

Katani was looking completely embarrassed—her partner Joe seemed to think this was a chance for slow dancing and kept trying to snuggle closer to her.

The one who seemed to be doing best was Avery. She and Dillon were cracking up, clearly enjoying themselves—much to Maeve's fury.

Jody called everyone to attention. "OK, now the box step is exactly that. Guys, hold your partners like this—hand on the small of her back, bodies straight, eyes on hers—"

Her—what? Charlotte thought, embarrassed beyond belief. Sammy stared straight into her chest, his face beet red, clearly not daring to breathe.

Jody showed them how to make a box with their feet. "Guys—step in to your partner, feet together, right foot right, feet together, right foot back, feet together," Jody chanted.

For the first ten minutes or so, there was lots of laughter and a few shrieks as toes got stepped on. But before too long, almost everyone seemed to have it. Jody said it was time to turn on some music and try to put it to a beat. Soon the well-known music to "Tea for Two" was blaring out on the sound system.

Charlotte stopped feeling mortally embarrassed, mostly because she knew Sammy was feeling a million times worse. He was actually really sweet, and he didn't step on her toes once. She was amazed that she was able to keep her feet in the right places, too. It was actually—she couldn't believe she was thinking this—kind of fun!

Maeve did her best to get the steps down without focusing on Riley. Pretend, she told herself. Pretend it's Orlando Bloom. *You will get through this, Maeve Kaplan-Taylor.* She had to wipe her hand a few times. But she felt bad about it, because Riley actually blushed. He seemed so embarrassed about it. "Sorry," he said, wiping his hands on his pants. "My hands ... sometimes sweat a lot."

"That's OK, Riley," Maeve told him. It was one of Maeve's deepest principles that "what comes around goes around." Which meant that if she were nice to Riley, Dillon would ask her to dance later on! The good thing was that Riley actually seemed to get this whole dancing thing. He hadn't stepped on her feet once.

Isabel was having the hardest time. Billy had two left

feet—though it felt more like eight. It wasn't just that he kept stepping on her—hard—and that her toes were bare in her strappy high heels. He was so clumsy that he kept whacking her into the couple behind them. And he didn't even seem to care. "Watch it," he kept saying to Isabel, as if it were her fault.

Katani discovered Joe wasn't that bad—once she got him to keep the proper distance, he was a good dancer, and pretty funny, too. She was also surprised to discover that she was actually having a good time.

As for Avery—well, she couldn't believe this was all there was to it. Making funny boxes with your feet—this was dancing? The actual steps were a piece of cake. The hard part was seeing the point. She had to admit that dancing wasn't all that bad.

Jody came around to offer encouragement or give advice as they finished off the lesson. She stopped to watch Dillon and Avery with a frown. "Try to loosen up," she advised Avery, shaking her arm a little to make it looser. "Try not to jump around so much, OK? Try to feel the music. Let it get you going!"

"I'll tell you where I'm going," Avery whispered as soon as Jody was out of earshot. "I'm going—to get out of here! And not come back!"

Dillon laughed, and Maeve, who happened to be dancing nearby with Riley, gave Avery a serious scowl. But Riley, who had got the hang of the box step really well, spun Maeve around in quite an elegant fashion. She looked up at him in surprise.

"OK, guys! Good work for the first class!" Jody called out, clapping her hands in front of Riley and Maeve. Then she signaled that the first part of the class had finished. "Help yourselves to refreshments, and after a short break, it's dance however you feel like it!"

Finally, Maeve thought, breaking free of Riley's damp hands and giving him the most gracious smile she could muster.

Finally, Isabel thought, rubbing one sore foot and backing off from Billy Trentini with a limp.

Finally, Charlotte thought, following Sammy over to the refreshments table where the difference in their heights didn't matter so much.

It looked like almost everyone was relieved for the break. Except, Maeve noted angrily, for Avery and Dillon. He'd apparently told her something hilarious, and they were so busy laughing together they didn't even seem to notice that the dance floor around them had completely cleared.

FOUL PLAY

"I just want to tell you," Maeve seethed to Avery as she stomped after her to the bathroom, "that I completely know what you're up to and I am not going to stand for it!"

"Great," Avery said mildly. "I have to put up with an hour of turning in circles on purpose, and my friend has gone whacko on me, too. A perfect end to a perfect evening."

"I just happen to know what you're doing with Dillon. You know I like him! He's—" Maeve struggled to think clearly. "He's—off-limits," she said weakly.

They had gotten to the bathroom and opened the door, and found it was packed with girls. Anna and Joline were holding court in front of the mirror, dragging out more makeup than would fill a counter at Bloomingdale's. "Doesn't this make my lips look totally full?" Anna was exclaiming, admiring herself in the mirror.

"Totally," Joline crowed, while three or four girls hung

around them admiringly.

"Forget it," Avery said, stepping back. "I hate bathrooms. Don't need one that bad anyway." She turned to look at Maeve. "Do we need mood management today," she added sarcastically. "You think I like Dillon? As in 'like'?"

Maeve stopped short. "Don't you?" she faltered.

"Nope. I don't 'like' anyone," Avery retorted. "Get a life, Maeve! Dillon and I are just friends!"

"But—" Maeve looked at her weakly. "But I heard you talking to Katani!" she cried. "Remember? You said—I heard you—that you couldn't believe he'd asked you. And then you asked her for help. And your parents didn't like it, and ..."

Avery stared at her, clearly not understanding. "What?" she demanded blankly. "Oh," she said at last. "That." She shook her head. "You are such a dufus, Maeve. The guy who asked me—that was my coach. It's a soccer thing. I can't really go into it right now, but trust me, it doesn't involve Dillon."

Maeve felt a little silly. "But—then—why did you ask Katani for help?"

"I asked Katani to help me design my blog. What did you think? That I was asking for dating tips?"

Maeve didn't tell Avery that that was exactly what she'd thought.

"Your what?"

"My blog. It's like a website, but cooler." Avery shrugged. "Maeve, you need some serious help. How come you torture yourself the way you do? The only one around here who thinks about liking guys 24/7 is you!"

Maeve's cheeks reddened. She felt really silly now. "Ave, I'm sorry," she said in a rush. "I don't know what I was thinking—I'm just—I don't know, when we were mad at each other I thought—"

"Never mind," Avery said. "Do me a favor. Help me find a bathroom that doesn't smell like a perfume factory." She coughed. "This place is bringing on an asthma attack. And I don't even have asthma!"

SLOW DANCE

For the first ten minutes of Free Choice, nobody danced at all. It was clearly torture for Maeve. "I want to ask him," she kept saying to the others, "but I can't until there's at least four other couples out there!"

Clearly everyone felt the same way. Finally, a tall, really cute guy from another school asked Joline to dance. Then Joe asked Katani. Before long, there were enough people out there that Maeve couldn't stand it anymore.

"I'm asking him," she announced. And off she went.

"You've got to admire her nerve," Avery said calmly, helping herself to some chocolate chip cookies.

Charlotte laughed. She relaxed for the first time in ages, forgetting all about England and her father and everything else. It was fun listening to the loud music and watching people having a good time. Henry Yurt was dancing with Betsy. Anna was dancing with Pete Wexler. Miraculously, Maeve was dancing with Dillon—and they even seemed to be having a good time.

She was so busy watching everyone else that she jumped when a voice near her said her name.

"Feel like dancing?" Nick asked tentatively.

"Sure," Charlotte said with a smile.

Just as they walked out on to the dance floor, the song ended.

"That's OK. We'll wait for the next one," Nick assured

her, and Charlotte nodded.

The next song started up, and Charlotte listened with a gulp. It was a slow dance.

"Still up for it?" Nick said lightly, reaching for her.

Charlotte gulped again. A few other couples were out on the dance floor, squeezing each other tightly. She saw Maeve hanging onto Dillon for dear life. "OK," she said uncertainly. She didn't have the faintest idea what to do next.

Nick put his arms around her. He felt much stronger than she would have guessed. And he held her very close. She could actually feel his heart beating through his jacket as he pressed her against him.

Charlotte rested her face against his chest. Everything around her seemed to fade out, until it was just her—and Nick. She had never slow-danced before, and she wasn't sure whether she liked it or not.

But she liked being close to Nick. It felt good. And, in a strange way, incredibly right.

CHAPTER 15

❧

THE MYSTERIOUS LETTER

FOR THE NEXT few days, everyone kept talking about the Wednesday night dance class. Joline managed to drop about a million hints about the cute guy who'd asked her to dance. "Of course, he noticed me right away," Charlotte heard her telling Anna and several other girls outside of their lockers. "You know how it is with chemistry. It just happens."

Charlotte hadn't seen or talked to Nick since Wednesday night. He wasn't in school on Thursday, which was a little weird. Maybe he caught a cold, she thought. *Or maybe he was sorry that he'd asked her to dance and was too embarrassed to run into her.*

Maeve wanted to go over and over every detail at lunch. "I can't stand waiting a whole month until the next class!" she wailed. She sneaked a look over one shoulder at Dillon's table. Now that Katani and Avery had come back to their usual spots, Dillon and Pete had a bunch of guys who were sitting with them—Clark, David, and Jameson, three guys who were on the J.V. football team with Pete. Not exactly an easy crowd to infiltrate.

"So, Ms. Rodriguez says that the editor from *The Sentinel* is coming in tomorrow morning," Katani told everyone, clearly eager to change the subject away from dance class. "Any of you guys submitting stuff?"

Isabel nodded. "I'm going to give my cartoon a try."

"I've decided I like freelancing," Avery announced. "I'm going to send my piece in as a Letter to the Editor. At first I was just annoyed that you have to check off that box about what race you are on school forms. But now that I've started doing research on the subject, I think the whole Census needs fixing." She popped her milk carton for emphasis, and Maeve giggled.

"You're such a radical, Ave," she said fondly.

"How about you, Maeve? How are the advice-to-the-lovelorn letters coming?" Katani asked her.

Maeve shrugged. "OK. I'm going to submit them, and see what the people at *The Sentinel* think." She studied her fingers, sighing. "Of course ... my mom thinks I'm over my head. But I don't care," she added emphatically. "I like writing advice letters."

Katani looked at her thoughtfully. "Maeve—how are your blankets coming along?" she asked. Not in a mean way, but as if she really wanted to know.

"I told you—they're kind of ... on the back burner." Maeve looked a little uncomfortable.

"You know," Avery said, sitting up a little and looking at Maeve. "I've been thinking about those blankets of yours, Maeve. It's maybe not as completely lame an idea as I thought at first."

"Gee, thanks," Maeve said. "You really know how to boost a girl's confidence, Avery."

"No, I'm serious. I saw this website when I was working

on my blog last night—it's called Project Linus, and they do something like you want to do. Only they give blankets to kids who are sick, not to the homeless." Avery grinned. "Remember Betsy and her Project Bread? We could call yours Project Thread." She started to crack up. "Get it? Thread? Sewing?"

"I get it." Maeve looked miffed. "Listen, I know it's a great idea. I just kind of ran out of ... skill." She shifted uncomfortably. "I'm all thumbs when it comes to sewing. Isabel can vouch for me. Tell them, Izzie. Tell them how every time I tried to sew a square I ended up making something that looked like a starfish."

"She's right," Isabel agreed. "She's pretty awful. I mean—sorry, Maeve, it's just that sewing doesn't come naturally to everyone," she amended hastily.

"Well, I think we should help," Katani said suddenly.

Maeve's eyes widened. "Help?" she echoed, as if she couldn't believe her ears.

"Like the little elves and the shoemaker," Avery sang out cheerfully. "Beacon Street Girls to the rescue!"

Charlotte laughed. "That's a great idea. Why don't we meet up in the Tower room after school today and see if we can turn this project around?"

Katani and Avery winked at each other. Charlotte got up to clear her tray, and Katani leaned forward to whisper to everyone else. "And that," she said, "will give us the perfect chance to plant our first 'surprise' for Charlotte and her father!"

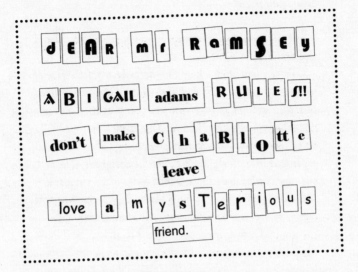

dEAr mr RamSEy

ABIGAIL adams RULES!!

don't make CHaRlotte

leave

love a mysTerious

friend.

Katani was the one to hide the note. All five girls were up in the Tower, Maeve's blanket project—such as it was—spread out all over the floor. Katani pretended that she wanted to get a glass of water.

She decided, after a good deal of thought, to hide the letter in the refrigerator—right on top of the salad greens. Her hope was that Mr. Ramsey and Charlotte would find it together—she remembered hearing Charlotte say that they liked to cook dinner together.

She wasn't sure what kind of impact it would have. But at least it might get Mr. Ramsey thinking a little!

❀

Charlotte's Journal
Thursday night

Tonight something really weird happened. Weird and wonderful.

First I have to back up and describe what the five of us were up to this afternoon in the Tower. Maeve's decided to try to get her blanket project going again—but she desperately needs help. Katani is amazing when she really decides to throw herself into something. She had us all organized in no time. She's doing the designing. The way she has it planned, there won't have to be very much sewing anymore. We're going to use fleece, which Katani says is really easy to work with. All Maeve has to do is to cut it with these fancy scissors that Katani says will make curly edges. If she wants to, she can sew on decorations— buttons, or ribbons, or little designs that Katani calls "appliqués."

Isabel and I are in charge of making signs, and helping Maeve to get in touch with a shelter in Brookline. And Avery is what she calls a "runner." Today that seemed to me like literally running around the Tower room chasing Marty. But eventually she'll help run errands, run things back and forth between our houses ... and run out for refreshments! Today she felt like she just had to run to Montoya's to see if they had any of those great fried cookies they make.

I was wondering if Nick was there but I didn't ask.

Anyway, it makes me so happy that the five of us are all together again. And I can tell Maeve is out of her mind with excitement that she's actually getting help with her blanket project. "Project Thread," as Avery keeps calling it, looks like it's really coming together.

Later Dad and I were making dinner together and he found this piece of paper curled up on top of the lettuce. He pulled it out, put on his reading glasses, and cleared his throat.

"Charlotte? Do you know anything about this?"

He showed me the note. It was in these funny little cutout letters, like the kind of thing you see on the news that ransom notes are written in. All the letters were squiggly and different sizes.

We both just stared at it. Dad could tell that I had no idea what it was.

"Did one of your friends leave this?" he asked.

I couldn't imagine any one of them doing that. It wasn't their style. They'd tell me, anyway. So I shook my head, wondering about Miss Pierce. But she wouldn't say our school "rules"—would she?

I even thought of Nick, and that made me blush. Right. Nick wasn't even in school today. How was he going to find himself in our kitchen—without me noticing?

I like the note, anyway. I taped it up on my wall so I could look at it. It reminds me of that scene in Charlotte's Web when they find in the spider web the letters Charlotte wrote: "Some Pig."

So I have a mysterious friend, too—just like Wilbur did. And whoever it is, my friend is trying to save me—just like Charlotte tried to save Wilbur!

CHAPTER 16

ↂ

EMERGENCY MEETING

FRIDAY MORNING in homeroom, Jennifer Robinson, a ninth grader and editor-in-chief of *The Sentinel*, came in to collect submissions from Ms. Rodriguez's homeroom. Jennifer was all energy—short, dark cropped hair, and funky purple glasses. She hopped on the desk in front of the class, swinging her legs as she talked.

"I want to thank you guys," she said, looking around the room. "Ms. Rodriguez told me that someone in here was the one who suggested changing the rules so that seventh graders could get involved. What a great idea!"

Isabel nudged Charlotte, who could feel her face turn hot and red.

"We're really excited to have your energy and involvement. We're going to read your submissions, and we'll post a list outside *The Sentinel* office next Friday letting everyone know how it works out!"

She hopped off the desk to gather up submissions. Charlotte fiddled with the button on her jean jacket. Part of her wanted to jump up and say, "Wait a minute! I changed my mind!" But what would be the point? Suppose Jennifer put her on the list, and she got to write for the paper—she'd be lucky to make it through orientation before it was time to resign.

She looked wistfully at the essay she'd written. She really liked it—and Ms. Rodriguez had liked it too. Oh well. Maybe I can give it to someone to read—in Oxford, Charlotte thought sadly, slipping it into her notebook.

She was so distracted, that she didn't even notice that the essay dropped as she was trying to get it into her binder. It fell down under her desk.

Isabel noticed, though. She reached down to pick it up for Charlotte, and was about to touch her shoulder to pass it back when she caught sight of Charlotte's title. Almost without meaning to, Isabel scanned the first few sentences that Charlotte had written. A shadow crossed her face.

She didn't hand the essay back to Charlotte. Instead, almost as if someone else were doing it, Isabel included Charlotte's essay with her cartoon, and raised her hand to signal to Jennifer that she had something she wanted to pass in.

And Charlotte's essay went right along with Isabel's cartoons—almost as if Charlotte had changed her mind and handed it in herself.

ભ

At lunchtime, Maeve passed a note to Katani under the table. "Second emergency meeting—this afternoon, at my house. Pass it on."

It wasn't easy finding a way to plan without Charlotte catching on. That girl was too quick. They managed to get the

❀

note from Katani to Isabel undetected. But Isabel slipped up passing it to Avery—Charlotte was halfway back from the drinking fountain—and Maeve had a weird feeling she'd seen.

If so, she didn't say anything. But she seemed a little funny for the rest of the lunch hour, and actually excused herself to go to the library and catch up on some homework.

"Ooops," Isabel whispered. "I guess I blew it."

"She won't mind when she finds out why," Avery said blithely. "It's all for a good cause."

Maeve wasn't so sure. "She seemed kind of upset, guys—"

"Listen," Isabel broke in. "I have to tell you what I did today in homeroom." She took a deep breath. "I hope this wasn't too terrible, but I had this great opportunity and I couldn't stand to waste it!" She told the other girls what had happened with Charlotte's assignment.

"You turned it in for her?" Avery's eyes were huge. "Isn't that—illegal?"

Maeve rushed to defend Isabel. "It's not illegal. Although ..." She looked worriedly at Isabel. "Isn't she going to freak when she finds out?"

Katani nodded vehemently. "She made it pretty clear that she didn't want to try out, Isabel. She's not going to be happy about this."

"We can say it was an accident—" Isabel faltered.

Avery seemed to come to a decision. "No. That's not right. We can't lie. We have to tell her the truth—that we did it on purpose," she announced. "We can use it as part of our plan. If she really gets on to the paper, that'll be one more reason to stay here and not to move. We can show Mr. Ramsey her name on the paper's staff!"

"OK, great," Katani said. "But now listen, we need to

meet again to figure out the next part of our strategy for Charlotte and her father. When's good for you guys?"

Maeve, of course, was booked solid. And Avery had soccer practice. The best they could come up with was Friday afternoon at Maeve's house.

"And remember—not a word to Charlotte!" Maeve reminded them as they got up to clear their lunch table. "If she asks anyone what you're doing, just come up with some sort of white lie!"

Katani:
Today's Horoscope

> *Virgo: Take charge, girl! Enough of sitting around and worrying from the sidelines. It's time to get life jumpstarted! Don't hold back for another minute!*
> *Lucky numbers: 11, 42*
> *Lucky relationship days: Saturday!!*

Katani's idea came to her in the middle of English class. She was looking out the window, enjoying the pleasant sound of Ms. Rodriguez reading Emily Dickinson's poetry, when it occurred to her that other kids at school might want to get involved with Project Thread. *We need helpers*—and other kids would probably get into this, she thought. Why not make it a bigger project, with more involvement?

Katani corralled Maeve at their lockers before gym. "All we need is to get a teacher to sponsor us. And we could even do it during study hall."

Maeve loved the idea. "You're brilliant, Katani. No wonder you want to run your own design company one day. You've got so much ..." Maeve paused. "Vision," she added breathlessly.

Katani looked through her perfectly organized locker, took out the notebook she needed, and smoothed her hair, checking her reflection in her locker mirror.

Maeve looked from the inside of Katani's locker to her own. "Why can't I be organized like you are?" she wailed. Her binder for the next period class was nowhere to be found, and papers were stuffed everywhere. "My mom's right," she said tragically. "I have ODD. Organizational Deficit Disorder."

"Your mom," Katani said, "should stop labeling people!"

Maeve glanced at her, surprised. "She can't help it, Katani. She just wants me to succeed," she said. "If I weren't so random about everything—if I were more like you—she wouldn't worry so much. She's afraid that I am not going to be able to get a job when I grow up."

"If you were more like me," Katani said firmly, taking Maeve by the arm, "you wouldn't be you. And that would be really sad."

Maeve's face brightened. "I never thought of it that way," she said.

"So," Katani continued. "Should we ask Ms. Rodriguez if she'll sponsor our blankets?"

"Oh, Katani, that's the best idea yet! Ms. Rodriguez is perfect!" Maeve exclaimed.

Katani could've hugged her. She loved Maeve's enthusiasm. Couldn't her mother see that Maeve's infectious excitement about everything she did was a million times more important than just being organized?

"Anyway," Katani continued, almost as if she were thinking out loud, "that's the whole point about being a team, Maeve. We all have different stuff we're good at. You're the one who thought of the blankets. And you're the one who's stuck to it and believed in it. All you need is a little teamwork to get the job done!"

Maeve was practically on cloud nine by the time they reached Ms. Rodriguez's classroom. She could hardly wait 'til Project Thread was underway, and they had their first batch of blankets ready to deliver to the shelter!

❧

All that week Charlotte was dragging. Nothing seemed to lift her spirits—not even Maeve's news that Ms. Rodriguez had agreed to sponsor their blanket project, and they were going to devote second period study hall to it until the blankets were done. Charlotte agreed to help, but her heart just wasn't in it. One more thing that I won't be able to see through, she thought miserably. Yes, she was thrilled to be able to work with her friends. But would she be around to deliver the blankets? Or would she and her father already be in England?

"Isabel," she said at the end of homeroom on Friday, "do you want to go to Montoya's after school today?" Charlotte hadn't seen much of Nick since Dance class. She was feeling a little shy to go to the bakery on her own, though. Going with Isabel would lift her spirits.

Isabel thought for a minute. "I'd—oops, I can't," she said suddenly. "I've got plans."

"Oh ..." Charlotte said slowly. "OK, another time."

She bumped into Maeve and Katani in the school's downstairs bathroom. Maeve was brushing her hair, trying to get a good look at it from the side. "D'ya think Dillon would help with the blanket-making?" she was asking Katani. "Hey, Char!" she said when Charlotte came in.

"Boys and blankets," Katani pronounced, "do not mix. Don't even bother asking, Maeve."

"Hey," Charlotte said, splashing some cool water on her face in an attempt to wake herself up a little. "Do you all feel like coming to Montoya's after school with me today? I could use some company."

Maeve and Katani caught each other's eyes.

"Can't," Katani said.

"Sorry, we're ... I mean I'm ... busy," Maeve mumbled.

Charlotte looked from one to the other. "You are?" she repeated doubtfully.

"Yep. It's ... I've got an appointment," Maeve blurted. It was completely obvious that she wasn't telling the truth.

"Me too!" Katani echoed.

Charlotte swallowed. Why weren't they telling her the truth? What were they hiding from her? "Never mind," she said, trying to sound nonchalant.

She almost bumped smack into Avery, who came leaping into the bathroom, skateboard in hand.

"Hey, Ave," Charlotte said half-heartedly.

"Are we still meeting later?" she heard Avery ask as the door closed behind her.

Charlotte's eyes filled with tears. It was clear her friends were all getting together—without her. It's probably because I'm moving, she thought miserably. They know that I won't be around for much longer, so what's the point in investing any more time in being friends with me?

It was the worst day of the worst week that Charlotte could remember in a long time. She just wanted to go home and crawl upstairs and lie on her bed with Marty. *At least he won't abandon me*, she thought.

"Phew," Avery said, closing the door to Maeve's bedroom. "It sure wasn't easy getting over here without Charlotte finding out."

"I hope she's OK," Maeve said worriedly. "She looked totally sad all afternoon."

"I know—she wanted me to go to Montoya's with her," Isabel said.

"Us too!" Maeve cried, looking at Katani.

"Well, we better come up with a good plan," Katani said.

"How about sending her dad some information on all the negatives of moving too much with teenaged kids?" Avery said. "If Mr. Ramsey is at all like my dad, he'd be into that. My dad loves statistics and figures of any kind."

"I kind of like that idea," Katani said. "We'll have to do some research. Who's up for that?"

"I'll do it," Avery said. "I'm on the Web all the time anyway, working on my blog. I can find out some stuff and write it up."

"Let's send it as an anonymous letter," Maeve said. "That's much more mysterious than getting email. And he's more likely to read it and pay attention to it."

"OK," Avery said. "I'll see what I can find, and let's talk online before I send it."

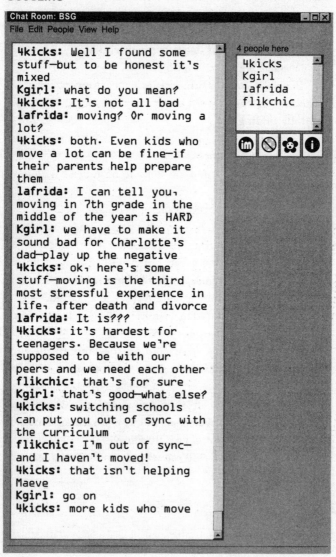

Chat Room: BSG

File Edit People View Help

4kicks: Well I found some stuff—but to be honest it's mixed
Kgirl: what do you mean?
4kicks: It's not all bad
lafrida: moving? Or moving a lot?
4kicks: both. Even kids who move a lot can be fine—if their parents help prepare them
lafrida: I can tell you, moving in 7th grade in the middle of the year is HARD
Kgirl: we have to make it sound bad for Charlotte's dad—play up the negative
4kicks: ok, here's some stuff—moving is the third most stressful experience in life, after death and divorce
lafrida: It is???
4kicks: it's hardest for teenagers. Because we're supposed to be with our peers and we need each other
flikchic: that's for sure
Kgirl: that's good—what else?
4kicks: switching schools can put you out of sync with the curriculum
flikchic: I'm out of sync—and I haven't moved!
4kicks: that isn't helping Maeve
Kgirl: go on
4kicks: more kids who move

4 people here

4kicks
Kgirl
lafrida
flikchic

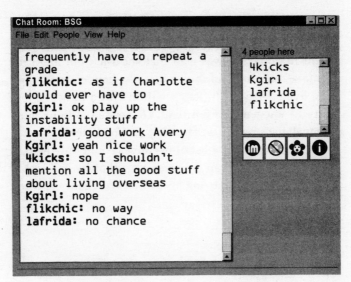

frequently have to repeat a
grade
flikchic: as if Charlotte
would ever have to
Kgirl: ok play up the
instability stuff
lafrida: good work Avery
Kgirl: yeah nice work
4kicks: so I shouldn't
mention all the good stuff
about living overseas
Kgirl: nope
flikchic: no way
lafrida: no chance

4 people here

4kicks
Kgirl
lafrida
flikchic

Dear Mr. Ramsey:

It has come to our attention that you are considering moving overseas. Again. You may or may not know some of the many problems that can come from moving with a teenager every year. Did you know that teenagers especially crave stability? They really need friendships more than ever at this age. This is not a good time to move every year if you can help it! Moving in the middle of the year is really hard. Your kid may be out of sync with the school she is moving to. Did you know that moving is the 3rd most stressful thing that can happen to a person after dying or getting divorced???

—A Friend

There! Avery thought, putting the letter into an envelope and picking her favorite stamp—the American flag. That ought to do it. She was glad that she'd left out all of the creative and powerful things that can happen to families who live overseas. Mr. Ramsey didn't need to hear about that—he knew all the positives. He needed to think more about all the stress he was heaping on Charlotte.

Putting together a list of negatives could only help. It was about time to drop the reverse psychology and let Mr. Ramsey know that moving again was just about the worst idea imaginable.

❧

CHAPTER 17

TALKING IT OUT

CHARLOTTE HADN'T planned on confiding in Nick. But she was feeling so blue on Friday afternoon that she stopped into Montoya's on her own, and before she knew it, she and Nick were having an iced hot-chocolate together—and more buñuelos.

"These things are addictive," Charlotte told him. They'd just come out of the oven and they were unbelievably good.

"My mom and my aunt used to make them for our family on Christmas morning," Nick said, smiling at her. "Here at the bakery, they're standard fare. But they still kind of remind me of Christmas!"

Charlotte sighed, almost unconsciously. Christmas. Where would she and her dad be then? Packing boxes to move to England?

"You OK, Charlotte?" Nick said. He looked uncertainly at the pastry she'd set down on her plate. "You don't have to finish that if you don't want to."

"Oh, it's not the pastry. It's delicious," Charlotte assured him. "It's just—well, everyone bagged me today," Charlotte said sadly. "Maeve, Katani, Isabel, Avery—they were all busy. Turns out, they all had plans—with each other. And they didn't include me."

Nick stared at her. "You're kidding me. You guys do everything together. They couldn't have left you out on purpose, Charlotte."

"They did!" Charlotte pushed her drink away miserably. "Trust me, they did. I don't know why—I have to admit it isn't like them ... But I think maybe it's because ..."

She looked uncertainly at Nick. "Well, because my dad and I may be moving to England," she said in a rush.

Nick looked upset. "Moving? But—you just moved. Here," he said emphatically.

"I know. My dad ... I don't know why this is, but he's ... I don't know, he just really likes moving, seeing new places, having adventures." Charlotte sighed again. It sounded so great when she put it that way. "I've always liked that too. It's just that things have changed somehow." Charlotte glanced uncomfortably at Nick. "I guess I'm not a little kid anymore, you know? I want to be able to stay in one place for a while."

Nick nodded. "I think I know how you feel. A lot of things are different when you get to junior high." He paused. "Are you sure your dad really wants to move? Have you tried to tell him how you feel?"

"Everything got all messed up," Charlotte said. "I wanted to tell him. But Isabel had this idea ... she called it 'reverse psychology,' and the plan was that I was supposed to really play up all the great things about moving. That way, my dad would realize that leaving Brookline and moving to Oxford wasn't such a good idea after all."

"Yikes," Nick said. "Reverse psychology. I tried that on my dad once. It never works."

"Yeah, I can see that now." Charlotte shook her head. "But by the time I'd done that, it seemed a little dumb to start confessing to my dad that I really don't want to move. I did try, but ..." She shrugged. "We ended up getting in a huge fight. Since then, we've just been saying regular things to each other. Like, 'What time is dinner?' And that's about it."

Nick looked closely at her. "Maybe you can still talk to him. Tell him how you feel. At least in my experience, that always works best."

Charlotte nodded. "You're probably right," she said. "I just have to get my courage up."

"But how could any of this have to do with Maeve and the rest of them? Why would they avoid you just because your dad wants to move?"

"I don't really know," Charlotte wailed. "But maybe they just figure that since I'm leaving anyway being friends with me is a waste of time and they should just forget about me now!"

"That's nuts," Nick declared. "I mean, I know girls can be weird. But not that weird."

Charlotte didn't say anything. She couldn't think of another reason to explain what had happened today and why her friends had all gone off together, without her.

℞

Mr. Ramsey came into the living room, where Charlotte was curled up with a novel. "Charlotte," he said, "I got this out of the mailbox today. Do you know anything about it?"

Charlotte got up and crossed the room to see what he was talking about. She caught her breath when she started to read the letter.

"Another one! Another—I don't know what to call them.

Like that note we found in the fridge," she murmured.

"Whoever wrote this went to some trouble," her father said. "They put some research into it ... and a stamp, even though they never put it through the mail."

Charlotte kept reading. She could feel her face growing warm.

"Is this stuff true? Does all of this really happen to kids who move too much?" she asked.

Mr. Ramsey sighed. "I think it could happen. It depends on so much. What the kid is like. What the family is like."

"Dad," Charlotte whispered, "do you think you and I could sit down and talk? I feel like there's so much we haven't been able to say to each other!"

Mr. Ramsey nodded. "You're right," he said, folding up the letter and slipping it in his pocket. Neither of them wanted to focus right now on who had sent the letter. It seemed like the most urgent thing was for the two of them to talk.

"It's not that I don't like the idea of England," Charlotte said carefully. "I do. I've always loved traveling to new places with you—we've had so many wonderful adventures! But when we came here, this seemed different to me. Special. Maybe because I was born here ... because you and Mom and I lived here when I was a baby ... it was like coming home."

A shadow crossed her father's face, the way it often did when she mentioned her mother.

"Don't you like living here, Dad?" Charlotte cried.

"I do," he said slowly. "In most ways, I do. But I have to admit that at times I've wondered if it wasn't a bit of a mistake, trying to come back to Boston." He swallowed, looking past Charlotte out the window into the late autumn night. "There are so many memories here," he said.

"But—aren't they good memories? And isn't it important

to have them?" Charlotte asked uncertainly. "That's part of why I want to be here, Dad! I love knowing that when I walk down the street here, I'm somewhere where Mom once walked!"

Her father was quiet. Charlotte thought she saw tears welling up.

"If only ..." He took off his glasses and wiped his eyes with his shirtsleeve. "If only she were still here," he whispered.

Charlotte took a deep breath. "Dad, we can't bring her back. But we can still make a home for ourselves here. We can make a real home, with roots. A place where we can celebrate holidays and have friends over and look forward to staying put for a while. A long while!"

Her father shook his head. "I don't know, Charlotte." He looked incredibly sad. "I know it may not be fair to you. But somehow ... moving is the only thing that makes the sadness stop hurting so much. I thought I could face it, coming back here. But I'm just not sure I can." He took Charlotte in his arms, hugging her tightly. "You know I don't want to hurt you! I'd do anything to make you happy! But I just don't know ... I don't know if I can do this, Char."

Charlotte sat up, trying hard not to cry herself. She had a huge lump in her throat, and her head was beginning to throb. "It's OK, Daddy," she said dully.

She couldn't believe that she was trying to comfort him. She felt so many different feelings at once. Always, for as long as she could remember, Charlotte had trusted that her father knew what was right. But this time was different. In her heart, Charlotte sensed that what her father was saying was wrong. Not that it wasn't painful to face the past—but she knew that he had to do it. Yes, it was hard to be back here, where they'd been a whole family once. Where her mother had been alive and well. But until her father could do this, Charlotte knew they would always be moving. She just had to find a way to show him that it was important to stay here ... to make a home again. She just had to.

4kicks: I hope he liked the letter
flikchic: me 2
Kgirl: it better make a difference
lafrida: yeah it better
flikchic: what's the next step?
4kicks: good point we need another plan
lafrida: a really BIG plan
flikchic: something that will make him see that they have to stay
Kgirl: what do you have in mind?
4kicks: I have 2 think
flikchic:so we should meet again
Kgirl: same time, next week?
lafrida: sounds good
flikchic: ditto
4kicks: ditto 2

Chat Room: BSG

File Edit People View Help

4 people here

4kicks
flikchic
Kgirl
lafrida

Charlotte's Journal
Monday afternoon

    So here's the strangest thing of all—today at school, everybody acted just like normal. Maeve was her usual bubbly self, and Katani was in a great mood—she loves this blanket project of Maeve's! Isabel was fine, and Avery was too. Now I don't know what to think. And they didn't avoid me at all. In fact, Avery kept saying that they really needed me to get in touch with the homeless shelter. Maeve and I are going to go there for a visit before her Hebrew class tomorrow.

    Was I just imagining things last Friday? Maybe I'm getting too sensitive—maybe all this worry about moving is making me see things that aren't there.

    Anyway, I'm so glad that things are back to normal. I need my friends more than I ever have.

 ....

```
Maeve:
Notes to Self


1. Talk to Hebrew School class about
   blanket project—tell them it's on,
   full steam!
2. Figure out stuff with shelter tomorrow
   afternoon.
3. Figure out an answer for Ask Maeve
   letter from the girl who feels like a
   failure.
4. Change I.M. away message!!!
5. Check and see if Dillon's online.
```

CHAPTER 18

❧

FINDING THE PAST

CHARLOTTE KNOCKED tentatively on the door to Miss Pierce's apartment. It was late afternoon, and sunlight was streaming in through the big bay windows when Miss Pierce opened the door.

"Charlotte! This is a nice surprise," Miss Pierce said, gesturing to invite her in. "I've just made a pot of tea—would you like some?'

Charlotte nodded, following Miss Pierce into her sunny kitchen. She loved the feel of it in here—bright yellow walls, ceramic of all colors on the farmhouse table, and classical music playing on the radio.

Miss Pierce had an old, soft sofa at one end of her kitchen, and Charlotte sank into it gratefully, taking the teacup her landlady offered her.

"This smells great—what is it?"

"Green tea. Calms the nerves and quiets the senses," Miss Pierce said, sitting down beside Charlotte with a smile. "Tea and yoga—those are my two favorite antidotes to the modern world."

Charlotte took a sip. The tea was delicious. She closed her eyes as she breathed in the aroma.

"It's nice to have you visit, Charlotte." Miss Pierce looked at her with affection. "How are things going with those lovely friends of yours? Spending much time up in the Tower these days?"

Charlotte shook her head. "To be honest, we've all been too busy. Maeve's got this big blanket project she's trying to pull together. Everyone's busy with school and afterschool stuff, and then ..." She set her tea down on the table. "Well, there's this stuff about me and my Dad, and the whole move to England."

Miss Pierce nodded. "I was wondering about that," she said gently. "But I didn't want to pry."

That was one of the things that Charlotte loved about Miss Pierce. She always let you say what was on your mind, instead of firing questions at you the way some grown-ups might.

"I've tried talking to my dad," she said unhappily. "But it's like he's got this big wall up. I'm so confused," she added, "because Dad was the one who talked so much about how great it was going to be for us being back in Boston. Last spring, when we started talking about moving here, Dad showed me all these pictures of the Public Gardens, and the magnolia trees blooming on Commonwealth Avenue downtown ... and sailboats on the river .... He was the one who kept talking about how important it was for us to be coming back here." Charlotte fought back tears. "Now that we're here, and I love it, he's ... I don't know ... it's like he doesn't want to be here. I just don't understand."

"Charlotte," Miss Pierce said softly, "I have a hunch. I may be wrong about this, but I think it may be that the way your father's behaving now has everything to do with just how much he wanted to come back."

"What do you mean?" Charlotte asked, confused.

Miss Pierce cleared her throat. "Tell me a little bit about what you remember about being here," she said. "Before."

"You mean, before my mom died?" Charlotte pushed her hair back, concentrating. "I don't remember that much. I was only four when she died. I remember ... there was a day ... well, I'm not even sure I remember this, or if it's just because I have this picture that I love so much, and I've looked at it so many times ... do you know how sometimes you can't tell if you're remembering the thing that happened or the picture of it?"

Miss Pierce nodded. "I know just what you mean," she said.

"Well, in my favorite picture, my mom is reading me a story. We're in this room—I guess it was in our old apartment, downtown. There's a big flowered chair, and a blue lamp next to it, and a cozy soft quilt. And in the picture I'm snuggled up with my mom and she's reading to me from *Charlotte's Web*." Charlotte paused. "That's my all-time favorite book," she added.

"It's one of my favorites too," Miss Pierce said.

"Anyway, that's one thing I remember. And another thing is walking with my mom and dad somewhere—I think we were near the swan boats," Charlotte said. "My mom was holding one of my hands and my dad was holding the other." She swallowed. "And they were swinging me. You know ... I'd jump up a little, and they'd swing me back and forth ..." Her eyes filled with tears. "It felt so good, holding onto both of them at once."

"Charlotte." Miss Pierce covered Charlotte's hand with hers. "Can you imagine how hard it might be for your father, coming back here and reliving all these memories? Maybe he didn't realize before you two moved back here how difficult it might be for him."

"But what's the answer? We can't just keep moving," Charlotte burst out. "He can't run away forever."

"I agree." Miss Pierce took a deep breath. "Charlotte, grown-ups don't have all the answers—just because they're older. Sometimes we need to be taught, too. Do you think you might be able to help your father?"

"How? I've tried," Charlotte began.

"I know you have. But you have to try again." Miss Pierce set her teacup down, thinking. "How about spending a day with your father—just the two of you? How about asking him to show you some of the places that were most important to you as a family when you lived here?"

Charlotte didn't want to hurt Miss Pierce's feelings, but she really couldn't see how that would help. "Wouldn't that just make it worse?" she asked.

"It's worth a try," Miss Pierce continued. "It may be that your father needs to confront exactly how difficult it is for him to be back in Boston, and why, before he's able to move on."

"OK," Charlotte said quietly. "I've tried reverse psychology, and that sure didn't work. And I tried telling him just how I felt, and that didn't work either! So maybe this will." She gave Miss Pierce a quick hug. "Thank you so much for talking with me. You have no idea how much better I feel. I hate just bottling stuff up ... and even though Marty is good company, he doesn't always have the best suggestions!"

Miss Pierce's eyes misted over. "Charlotte Ramsey," she whispered, as Charlotte got up and set her teacup on the counter. "You have no idea what a joy it is for ME."

❀

"I've got my fingers crossed!" she called out as Charlotte let herself out.

"Thanks!" Charlotte called back. It was funny to think that she used to be afraid of her landlady. Now it almost felt like Miss Pierce was like her adopted grandmother!

ᘓ

"So, we need an idea. An all-out, show-stopping, this-is-it kind of idea," Maeve said, pacing around her bedroom with a frown.

Isabel was lying on the carpet, doodling in her notebook. "Think," she instructed herself. "Think, think, think."

Katani had her head in her hands, tapping her fingers.

"The only way to get a good idea is to get the blood flowing to your head," Avery announced, pushing aside a box marked "Extra Fabric" so she could do a handstand against Maeve's bedroom wall.

"Avery, you're weird," Maeve said affectionately.

The four girls had been trying for the past half-hour to think of some grand finale to finish up their "Keep the Ramseys in Boston" scheme. So far, no great ideas were forthcoming.

"I've got it!" Avery said, rolling down from the headstand. Her face was pink from being upside-down. "Why don't we send a letter from Oxford apologizing to Mr. Ramsey and explaining that someone else took the job instead of him?"

"I don't know, Avery. I think that's a little ..."

"Illegal," Katani finished for Maeve. "And definitely not right."

Avery sighed. "Technicalities," she objected. "Come on, guys. Can you do any better?"

"I feel like we need to do something dramatic," Maeve said.

Katani nodded. "Something different. Not a letter this time."

"Maybe," Isabel said slowly, looking at the doodle she'd finished, which was looking more and more like a chair, "we could try to do something to the Tower. Transform it, somehow. And then invite Charlotte and her father to come up there ..."

"You know," Katani said, looking at Isabel with interest. "That's actually kind of a good idea, Isabel."

Isabel's cheeks pinkened. It was the first time that Katani had actually said something really nice to her. "You think so?" she asked.

Maeve snapped her fingers. "I've got it!" she cried. "Transform the Tower room into a memory! A place that Charlotte and her dad used to love, right here in Boston!"

"How do we do that?" Avery demanded. "How on earth do we know what kind of memories Charlotte and her dad have?"

"Pictures, silly," Maeve told her. "We find a picture, and we make the Tower room look just the way the place in the picture looks. That way when Mr. Ramsey sees it, he'll feel really at home!"

"This is good. I think this is really good," Katani breathed.

"OK, Isabel. You're new," Maeve said, getting excited. "So you have the perfect excuse. You go over to Charlotte's house and figure out a way to get her to show you some old pictures. Say ... I don't know, you'll think of something. Then all you have to do is sneak one out."

"And we'll use it as our blueprint! The Tower Makeover!

✿

I love this—our very own *Trading Spaces*!" Katani cried.

Avery grinned. "And if it doesn't work, I'll write to Mr. Ramsey and tell him Oxford is shutting down," she said cheerfully.

The four girls looked at each other. They had a plan. Now all they needed was the perfect photograph to use as a model.

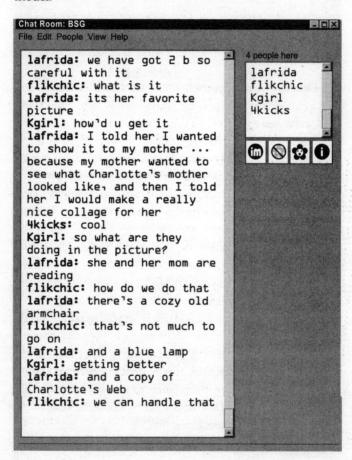

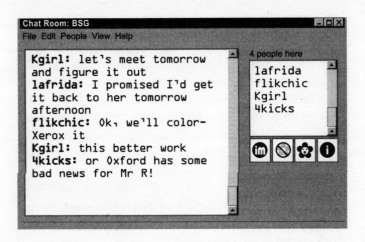

Chat Room: BSG
File Edit People View Help

4 people here

Kgirl: let's meet tomorrow
and figure it out
lafrida: I promised I'd get
it back to her tomorrow
afternoon
flikchic: Ok, we'll color-
Xerox it
Kgirl: this better work
4kicks: or Oxford has some
bad news for Mr R!

lafrida
flikchic
Kgirl
4kicks

❧

By the next afternoon, the girls had a color copy of Charlotte's photograph—and Isabel had safely returned the picture to Charlotte, assuring her that her scrapbook was coming along beautifully. She had told Charlotte that she was making her a collage scrapbook with memories of her friends and experiences in Boston as a farewell present. "I can't wait to show it to you—as soon as it's done!" she added.

The girls grabbed each other in the corner across from their lockers to pore over the picture.

"We can use the Lime Swivel. It's already up there, and we'll cover it with material," Katani whispered.

"You love that chair, don't you?" Maeve said sympathetically. Katani nodded. The Lime Swivel had belonged to her great-grandfather, who had given it to Miss Pierce and her Grandma Ruby when they were little. Every time she saw it in the Tower, Katani felt a connection to her family's past.

"I have a lamp that looks a little bit like that. It's up in our attic. My mom would never miss it," Avery said.

"We can 'borrow' Charlotte's copy of *Charlotte's Web* the next time we go over there," Maeve added.

They were really getting into the idea now. "I think this could really work," Isabel said excitedly. "We'll set the whole thing up ... make it look exactly like it does in the picture."

"Uh ... minus Charlotte. And her mom," Katani pointed out.

Isabel nodded. "Right. I know. But I mean, we'll have the whole scene set just right. And then we'll invite Charlotte and her Dad up, and we can have a big sign over the door that says 'Welcome Home,' and—"

"Sshhh. She's coming!" Avery hissed.

Operation Tower Room Makeover was going to have to wait—for now.

❧

"Do you realize," Maeve said the next afternoon, "that thanks to all of you, we are actually going to be able to deliver our first batch of blankets to the shelter next week?"

Room 206 had been renamed the "Project Thread" room—at least by Avery. It wasn't clear if anyone else had an actual name for it. But it had become the place to come during study hall.

Ms. Rodriguez had helped to get the word out. Jennifer had also helped by posting an ad outside *The Sentinel* office. "Interested in helping a group of seventh graders make blankets for kids in need? Drop by room 206 during study hall and join the fun!"

And it really was fun by this point. Katani was an amazing force when it came to organizing people. She had one group working on cutting out fleece blankets in every color imaginable—pastels for babies, bright colors for toddlers, and wonderful, unusual shades for older kids. Teal, purple, and cranberry were Katani's personal favorites. This girl was born to rule a corporate empire!

Maeve had a row of boxes filled with custom decorations —stripes, appliqués, badges, and even buttons—so kids could customize their blankets. Then the edges needed to be finished—one whir of Katani's sewing machine did the trick. The finished blanket needed to be folded and sorted it into one of the waiting bins—one marked "infants and babies," one marked "toddlers," and one marked "big kids!"

"I like this one," Avery said, picking up a red and navy blue blanket from the big kids' box that had a Red Sox badge sewn on it. "Can you guess who made it?"

"That couldn't possibly be yours now, could it?" Katani said dryly.

Maeve's personal best was a soft pink baby blanket that she had decorated with bright pink hearts all around the border. "I call this one baby love," she sighed, wrapping herself up in it.

"I can't believe how many we've got already," Isabel said, looking with amazement at the stacked bins. "Maeve, have you guys talked to the shelter about dropping these off?"

"Next Friday," Maeve said proudly. "My dad said he'd take us over in his van. So we can all go."

She looked at Katani, suddenly feeling shy. "The director of the shelter wants to meet all of us. She's really excited. Katani, I told her that we couldn't have done it without you setting up all of this ..."

"Maeve," Katani said firmly, "this is a team project, OK? We're all in it—and we've all worked hard. But you were the

❖

one who got it started."

Maeve was completely choked up. She didn't know why the blanket project had come to mean so much to her—but she knew it had. She also knew she hadn't been putting as much time as she should have lately into studying. And for the second time, she'd had to cancel a session with her tutor—just to get the blankets done. She hoped this wasn't going to be a disaster ... Especially with another big math test coming up.

But, the blankets mattered to Maeve—more than she'd ever realized. What she was feeling, she realized suddenly, was *pride*.

She had started the blanket project thinking that it would be great to help other people. And she had. But the funny thing was that she really felt like she had helped herself the most. It felt good, having done something useful. Something she could be proud of. And the best part was sharing it with her best friends.

CHAPTER 19

❧

A DAY OF MEMORIES

Charlotte's Journal

I was kind of surprised by dad's reaction when I suggested that we spend the day together on Saturday. I'm not sure what I was expecting. I guess since he and I have been getting mad at each other lately, I was half afraid that he might make an excuse to get out of it. And I know he has a lot of papers to grade, but he actually seems really excited about it. I told him that I wanted to see the house where I was born, and places that he and mom used to go. And the swan boats—he always used to tell me about the swan boats when we were on our houseboat last year.

At first he seemed surprised. Then he started to warm up to the idea. He said that he hadn't been back to any of those places since we moved here. And this seems like a great time.

So we made a date. Saturday morning, we'll get up early. We'll catch the trolley and go all the way down Beacon Street together into Boston. We'll have breakfast at a café on Newbury Street where he and my mom used to have coffee all the time. We'll walk around the garden and go see the swan boats—and even ride one if they haven't shut down for the winter. And then my dad says he'll take me to 170 Arlington Street, where he and mom were living when I was born.

It's too cold out tonight to sit on the balcony. I have to look for the stars from inside.

I've been reading up on Orion. There are different stories about him, but in most he is a hunter who was punished because he made the gods jealous. The Greeks thought that it was Apollo who was jealous because Artemis, Apollo's sister, loved Orion. After he died, Artemis put him up in the sky so she could always see him.

I've always loved Orion. I like the fact that he gets brighter as the days get shorter. And I love the names of the stars that make up his belt: Alnitak, Alnilam, and Mintaka. Miss Pierce told me all about them—she used to study them when she worked at Hubble. I think if Marty could have puppies we should name them after Orion's stars. What's amazing is that it turns out that the third star isn't a star at all, but a nebula. That's a kind of vapor filled with lots of stars. Some of them may even be forming their own solar systems, but from this far away we can't see that.

Lots of things are like that. They look one way from far away, and another way up close. For some reason, looking at the stars in Orion's belt makes me think about dad and what it's been like for him moving back to Boston. He's like one of those stars in a nebula—trying to make a whole new solar system of his own ... sort of.

I feel like kissing dad goodnight. When I pull my shade down I realize something. I'm not mad at him anymore. Even if we have to move back to England, I think I kind of understand.

Saturday turned out to be one of those golden, Indian summer days that come sometimes in New England in the late fall. On the Weather Channel everyone was saying that it was a record 68 degrees! Charlotte only needed a light jacket. Newbury Street was filled with people outside enjoying the weather—couples walking with their arms around each other, college kids shopping. It was nice sitting with her father outside. "This almost reminds me of Le Deux Garçons in Paris," she told her father. That had been their favorite café. Sometimes they managed to spend all morning there—Charlotte with a novel to read, and her father with *Le Monde*, the French newspaper he loved so much.

He laughed, putting aside his menu. "Paris prices, too!" Then he looked at Charlotte with a smile. "Your mom and I came here with you when you were a baby. We used to push you back and forth in your stroller to help you fall asleep. And your mom always ordered the same thing—an almond croissant and a café au lait. And," he added, remembering, "she always insisted on pulling the almond filling out from the middle of the croissant and eating that first!"

"That's what I do!" Charlotte cried. "I do that with any kind of food that has something gooey in the middle!"

"So there you go," her dad grinned. "Must be genetic."

The rest of the morning sped by. They walked for a while on Newbury Street before heading to the Public Garden. The swan boats were closed down for the season, but her father showed her just where they were, and they sat together on a

❁

bench for a while and watched people jog past. Charlotte saw a young family with a baby girl in a stroller. They look like we must have, she thought. We must've looked like that. She caught her father's eye and she guessed that he was thinking the same thing.

"Hey," he said gruffly, getting to his feet. "How about heading over to Arlington Street? Should we see if the old place is still standing?"

☙

Miss Pierce opened the door, looking with a smile at Maeve, Katani, Avery, and Isabel. When they had approached her last week to ask her to help them with their Tower Makeover, she had had some misgivings. But Maeve could talk a rock into doing what she wanted, as Avery put it. And by the time the girls were done with their campaigning, they had Sapphire Pierce firmly on their side.

"Now, Charlotte and her dad should be out all day—I know they have dinner reservations at about 7 o'clock. So you four shouldn't have any interruptions," she said. Marty started jumping wildly around their feet, and Miss Pierce laughed. "At least, not from any human beings. Marty—I can't help with."

Maeve led the way up to the Tower, carrying the color copy with her. Katani had her measuring tape and her sister's digital camera, and Isabel had a notepad and her sketching pens.

Avery saw herself as designated furniture-mover. "Here! We can move this over here—and this over here ..." She started dragging furniture from one place to another, before Katani held up one hand.

"Avery, remember—we're only planning today! Save

your strength for next week, when we actually do the heavy-lifting."

For the next few hours, the girls worked together like crazy, planning the best way to make the Tower look like the cozy nook in Charlotte's photograph. Katani measured the old barber's chair that the girls had found up in the Tower months ago. "If I get stuffing material, we can cover this in it—and add fabric. I've seen some that looks almost exactly like the fabric in Charlotte's picture on sale at the place where my mom and I go for sewing supplies."

Isabel sketched out the room as they talked. "What do you guys think?" she asked, holding up her drawing.

"It's going to work," Maeve said judiciously, looking around her. "Now all we have to do is make it happen, and get Charlotte and her dad up here to see what we've done!"

CR

No. 170 Arlington Street was an old brownstone building just between Commonwealth Avenue and Clarendon Street. In front of the house, a small dogwood tree stood in a well-tended garden behind a low wrought-iron fence. Charlotte and her father stood on the sidewalk, looking up at the building.

"I can't believe it." Her father was excited. "See that star sticker on the third floor window? That was your bedroom. Your mother put that sticker there when you were two. We'd been to the Planetarium in New York, and you wanted that sticker so badly." His eyes misted over. "Wow," he said at last. "How did that manage to survive, after all these years?"

"Dad," Charlotte said, squinting up at the windows. "You think we could ring the doorbell and ask to go inside?"

He hesitated. "I don't know—" He looked at her

uncertainly. "Part of me doesn't want to," he added in a low voice.

"Please." Charlotte's voice sounded urgent. As soon as she said it, she realized—she needed to see the apartment.

He looked closely at her, and then seemed to come to some sort of decision. "OK," he said. "Let's try."

They walked up the path together, and Charlotte rang the buzzer next to the button that said "Apartment #3." After a few minutes, a voice came out of the speaker next to the buzzer.

"Who is it?" A nice, pleasant-sounding voice. A woman, pretty young.

"We ... uh, I'm Richard Ramsey, and I'm here with my daughter Charlotte. We used to live in your apartment. Years ago, when she was a baby. She was hoping ..." Mr. Ramsey hesitated. "We were hoping we could come up," he said finally.

"Just a minute." Charlotte could hear some voices—a man's, a kid's. Then the woman came back. "Sure, come on up!" She sounded nice.

Once they'd been buzzed in, a change seemed to come over Charlotte's father. The hallway was dim and cool, with big black and white tiles and an old-fashioned elevator—the kind with gates that you pulled closed yourself. The walls were covered with flocked crimson wallpaper—very Victorian. Charlotte didn't feel anything—no memories of this place. But her dad looked like he was in a trance. She followed him up the stairs, watching him closely.

Four people were living in their old apartment now. Beth, the mom, looked like she was about thirty. She had a short, angular haircut and several pierced earrings in each ear. Her husband, Josh, had a ponytail and was carrying one of their two little kids in his arms. They seemed happy to meet Charlotte and her dad, and didn't mind at all if they looked around.

Charlotte kept waiting to feel something—some kind of memory. It was a nice apartment. There was a kitchen, a living room, and two bedrooms—one pretty good-sized. The door to the second bedroom was closed. "Nat is asleep," Beth said with a smile, pointing at that door.

They ended up spending more time there than Charlotte had expected. Beth and Josh were both writers, and they knew someone who taught with Mr. Ramsey at B.U., and before Charlotte knew it, they'd offered them tea and they were all sitting together at the table. It was nice, but she couldn't help feeling disappointed. This was the apartment where she lived for the first four years of her life—and it didn't trigger anything. No memories. Her dad, on the other hand, was exclaiming over every last thing—the windows, the views, the light, the shape of the kitchen counter. He loved being there, it was clear.

Just when they were about to leave, a baby started howling from the room with the closed door. "That's Nat," Beth said with a laugh. She looked at Charlotte. "Want to come with me to get him?"

Charlotte shrugged and nodded, following Beth as she opened the door to the second bedroom.

She blinked for a minute, getting used to the dim light, She could see the star sticker on the window. Then she looked around, and a feeling swept over her—it was almost like being dizzy, but more powerful.

This was the room in her picture.

Some things were changed, but the wallpaper was still the same. Over there, where Nat's crib was—that was where the stuffed armchair had been. Where she'd sat with her mother—not just that one time, but hundreds of times. The smell ... Charlotte half-closed her eyes, breathing it in. A mixture of old wood and a faint, deliciously musty smell. The light fixture on the ceiling ... the closet doors ... the little built-in windowseat ... It was all there.

We lived here, Charlotte thought wonderingly. Dad and I—and mom.

She walked over to the window and touched the star sticker with one finger.

"Charlotte? You okay?" Beth asked gently.

Charlotte nodded. She didn't turn around just yet. But strangely enough, she was fine. She felt so many different things all at once that it was hard to put a name to them all. Through the rush of emotions she was experiencing, she was aware of how solid the old oak floor felt underneath her. As if she had something strong to stand on—something that would never let her fall.

◈

"OK, guys. Done!" Maeve said later that afternoon, as the girls began packing up all of their stuff.

They had a design, and now they had a plan, too.

Next Saturday, Miss Pierce was going to figure out a scheme to get Charlotte and Mr. Ramsey out of the house again. "Don't worry, I'll think of something," she had promised the girls. While they were out, the four of them would spring into action and make over the Tower room. When they were done, they were going to leave a note in the Ramseys' apartment, telling them to go up to the Tower.

"And that," Avery asked skeptically, "is supposed to change Mr. Ramsey's mind about moving? Just like that?"

She snapped her fingers.

"Don't you get it, Avery? It's all about his *emotions!*" Maeve cried.

"I don't know," Avery said, shrugging. "Maybe I'm not 'emo' enough for you guys. But I'm happy to move furniture, anyway. It's good for upper-body strength."

"You are so unsentimental," Katani chided her. "Come on. Let's go get something to eat. I'm starving."

"I'm gonna take Marty for a run in the park—I'll catch up with you all later," Avery said as she snatched up Marty. "You, me, and the Frisbee. Right little buddy?" Way over the top with excitement, Marty thumped his tail madly against Avery's arm.

Maeve took a last look behind her as they closed the door to the Tower room. Well, this place had worked in special ways before, she thought, remembering how it had brought the Beacon Street Girls together in the first place. Why couldn't it work its magic one more time?

CHAPTER 20

❧

MAKING THE GRADE

"I HAVE news," Ms. Rodriguez told her homeroom on Monday morning. "Jennifer sent me an email this morning. *The Sentinel* has posted the new staff list outside their offices. After class, you can all check and see the results."

This announcement created a loud buzz, as everyone had to speculate about whether they'd really taken everyone who'd tried, or who might not have made it. Ms. Rodriguez had to call several times for everyone's attention.

"We have several more announcements," she told them. "Please—hang in there!"

She motioned to Maeve to come to the front of the room.

"Maeve wants to tell everyone about the work she's been doing for a local homeless shelter," Ms. Rodriguez continued. "Maeve—go ahead! The floor is all yours!"

Maeve hurried up to the front of the room, hesitated, and then launched into the speech she'd practiced several times last night with her dad. "So, we've started working on a project to make blankets for homeless kids in a shelter in Boston. It's called Jeri's Place. It's a shelter that provides a place to stay for women and children for as long as they need. They definitely need stuff for kids, and they're really excited to be getting our blankets." Maeve paused. "Anyway, originally we were just going to do this one time, but it's turned out to be really fun, and now we're thinking that we might try to keep it going even after we make our first delivery. So if anyone else wants to join us, come to Room 206 during second-period study hall."

Lots of excitement greeted this announcement, and Dillon gave Maeve a high-five as she walked back to her seat. She could feel her face turning pink. Now, whoever could've guessed that, she thought. Here she'd tried to flirt with Dillon about a million times—without results. But when she got up to make an announcement about the blankets—the one time that Dillon was actually not on her mind—he noticed her!

Weird, she thought, sliding into her desk and giving Charlotte, Isabel, Katani, and Avery a thumbs-up sign. Guys are definitely weird.

◌ℜ

The crowd in front of *The Sentinel* office was three deep.

"Go ahead," Charlotte said to Maeve and Isabel. "I'll wait for you here."

But she got swept along with them to the front of the crowd as others moved up behind her to get a look at the list.

"Yay! I made it!" Maeve exclaimed, running her finger down the list to Kaplan-Taylor. "You're on, too," she assured Isabel, pointing to her name.

Everyone was really excited. *The Sentinel* had accepted everyone who tried out, but some people had been placed in a group called "writers in training," and others were full

✿

writers or even editors.

"Hey, Charlotte. You got Feature Writer!" Maeve exclaimed. "You deserve it," she added loyally.

Charlotte stopped short. She followed Maeve's finger—and sure enough, there was her name, in bold block print. Charlotte Ramsey—Feature Writer.

"That's—that's a mistake," she said, her mouth dry as cotton. "I didn't submit anything."

Maeve and Isabel looked at each other. Neither of them said anything.

"I'll go find out what happened. It must just be an accident," Charlotte said again. It was hard to push through the crowd, and people kept saying "congratulations" to her over and over again.

How embarrassing! How was she going to explain to people that it was just an error?

Jennifer was on one of the newspaper computers, frowning at the layout for this week's newspaper. *The Sentinel* came out on the last Friday of every month, and on printing weeks, like this one, she was pretty busy. "We have to do something about this font," she was muttering to herself as Charlotte came in.

She looked up at Charlotte, trying to place her. "Here to help?" she asked.

"Uh—no, not really. I mean, I'd like to ..." In fact, the newspaper office looked exactly like the sort of place Charlotte loved best. "Jennifer, I'm Charlotte Ramsey, and I think—"

"Charlotte Ramsey!" Jennifer exclaimed. She put her hand out to shake. "Nice to meet you, and welcome to *The Sentinel*. We're so excited about your article. We really need a new feature writer, Charlotte. In fact, come have a look. I'm just laying it out right now!"

Charlotte gulped. "My—my piece? You mean—" She hurried around to look at the computer monitor. Sure enough, there it was—laid out on the screen. Jennifer was adjusting the font size of the headline and playing with Charlotte's name. Charlotte couldn't believe her eyes. The piece looked wonderful set in print. Maybe I just shouldn't say anything, she thought. Just let her print it, and not say a word.

But that wasn't honest. She hadn't submitted it to the paper. She hadn't tried out, and it wouldn't be fair to pretend that she had.

"Jennifer, I don't know how this happened. I didn't submit this. It must've—I don't know how it got to you," Charlotte stammered.

Jennifer pushed her purple glasses up on her nose with a frown. She pulled away from the computer, studying Charlotte for a minute. "You're kidding," she said at last. "Wow. This is a first. We've had kids who begged us to put their stuff in, and we had to say no. But we've never had this happen!"

Charlotte didn't know what to say.

"So—are you saying you don't want to be on the staff?" Jennifer asked at last.

Charlotte took a deep breath. "I did want to. More than anything. I was actually the one who wrote the Change a School Rule letter asking Ms. Rodriguez why seventh graders couldn't be on the paper. But then ... my dad is a writing teacher. We're new here, and he started talking about taking a job in England next semester, and it just didn't seem fair to try out."

"Fair? Not fair to us?" Jennifer asked. She had a straightforward manner that Charlotte really liked.

"Maybe. And not fair to me," Charlotte said in a small voice.

Jennifer folded her arms. "Are you definitely moving?"

"I think so. Not definitely. But probably."

Jennifer kept looking at her. "Do you want to work for the paper until you move?"

Charlotte took another breath. "Yes," she said. "I'd love to!"

"Good. Case settled. We don't mind how your piece got to us," Jennifer added, "although from your point of view, I can see why you might want to figure that out! But we're happy to have you on staff for as long as you're here. Don't worry about not being fair, Charlotte. Anyway, journalists often end up traveling a lot." She laughed. "Maybe if you end up moving, you can be a foreign correspondent—you can send us features from England!"

Charlotte felt elated like a huge weight had been lifted off her shoulders. She had wanted so badly to be on the paper. Jennifer's easy-going, yet serious manner made anything seem possible. She was still mystified about her piece—who had turned it in? How had it ended up in the pile on Ms. Rodriguez's desk? She remembered that she had specifically put it in her notebook—she was sure of that! How did it get here?

But the main thing was, she was on the paper—Charlotte was a Feature Writer!

"So, can we run this on Friday? We love this piece," Jennifer said.

Charlotte looked again at the monitor. This piece had felt so personal to her. She hadn't really wanted to share it. But that was before ... Before she'd gone with her dad to Arlington Street. Before she'd seen the room where she was a baby. Before she became a 'Feature Writer' for *The Sentinel*.

"Go ahead," Charlotte said. Wasn't that the point of

writing, anyway?—sharing what you felt with other people?

❦

Maeve had felt like she was practically floating all day. Not only had Dillon given her that high-five in homeroom, but he'd actually stopped to talk to her after class. "That blanket thing sounds cool," he'd said to her. "Nice going, Maeve." And Riley gave her a thumbs up as she walked by his desk. Maeve noticed that he had cut his hair. He looked kind of cute.

Then, to make life even better, there was her name on *The Sentinel* list. "Ask Maeve" was really going to happen! She almost had to pinch herself to believe this was real. Writing had always been a struggle for Maeve, and this was the first time she could remember a chance to write that she was excited about. Really excited about.

Then, during second-period study hall, people kept coming in to oooh and ahhh over the blankets. Even Anna and Joline stopped in—though of course, they didn't stay long. Maeve felt practically like a celebrity.

Her good mood lasted almost all day—until math. Mr. Sherman handed back tests at the end of the hour, but he didn't give Maeve hers. Not a good sign.

"Maeve, can you stay after for a minute?" he said in his "I'm-trying-to-be-casual-but-there's-actually-a-big-problem-here" kind of voice.

So when everyone else filed out of the classroom, Maeve stayed at her desk, palms damp and mouth dry. She hated this feeling. She could remember dozens of other times just like this—sitting at her desk and sweating, waiting for the inevitable. "Maeve, I don't know what happened." "Maeve, I'm disappointed ..." "Maeve, I'm concerned." All different

❀

ways of saying the same thing. Her heart sank.

Mr. Sherman approached her, pulling a chair up to sit near her. He took out her test. Maeve gasped. She knew she was in trouble. But—zero? A big fat red zero on top of her test? She'd never gotten all the answers wrong before. Never.

"We need to talk about this," Mr. Sherman was saying. He was actually being nice. Maeve could tell that he was trying to soften the blow and make her feel better. But she could barely hear what he was saying.

She heard the last part, though. "Ask your mom and dad to look this over tonight, and have them sign it and bring it back tomorrow." Maeve knew that teachers didn't do it to be horrible. They were required to by law or something. It meant that if a kid was flunking out, they couldn't keep pretending that everything was OK to their parents. Some parent had sued once, and now the school had this policy— tests with grades of "D" or lower needed to be sent home and signed by parents.

For a brief, wild moment, Maeve imagined signing the test herself. Or getting one of her friends to do it. But she knew she couldn't. She was terrible at math, but she wasn't a liar.

She could hardly remember the feeling of euphoria she'd had before math class. Now it felt like she could barely crawl through the door. She didn't even answer when Avery started bounding after her, asking her if everything was OK.

Everything was not OK. How on earth was Maeve going to explain this latest disaster to her mother?

Ꮕ

"This is unacceptable!" Maeve's mother shouted. "I told you that you were over-extended. But you and your father wouldn't listen to me." They were in the kitchen, Maeve's test lying on the table, face down. Her father had turned it over. He didn't want that big 0 staring at them the whole time, Maeve thought sadly.

"Mom, I know. I'm not happy about it, believe me. I'm the one who failed the test—not you."

This didn't seem to make her mother feel any better. "Maeve, you don't have to be rude," she cried. "We have a problem here, OK? And we need to figure out a way to deal with it!"

"I just don't understand ... I mean I've never gotten a zero before." Maeve said as she hung her head.

Sam wandered into the kitchen, curious about all the yelling. "What's up?" he asked.

It was an innocent enough question, but Maeve really didn't want her little brother in here, witnessing her total humiliation. "Get lost, Sam," she snapped.

"Maeve! Leave your brother out of this!" Her mother was really getting mad now.

"That's what I'm trying to do. He shouldn't be here," Maeve said, fighting for control.

"Maeve's right," her father cut in.

Then Maeve's mother turned on him. "That's all you ever do! Take her side! That's not exactly helpful."

"I'm just saying that Maeve's right; that this is a private conversation. Sam, do us a favor—"

"I'm going up to my room anyway," Sam said. "I've got homework," he added.

Was it Maeve's imagination or was he taunting her? Perfect little Sam. Of course he would never fail a test. Pigs would fly before Sam ever got less than a "B" on anything!

Maeve's mother was pacing back and forth in the kitchen. Pacing was not a good sign. It meant that she was

✿

not only mad, but that she had a plan in mind. Maeve felt herself tuning out, the way she did when she couldn't take her mom's disappointment. She heard little snippets. "Cut some after-school activities—less time on the computer—take away I.M. so she isn't distracted ..."

Maeve felt tears begin to slide down her cheeks. Her mom sat next to her and put her hand on Maeve's. "This isn't about punishment, sweetie," she said. She actually sounded nice, which was even worse. "It's just that I want you to be able to handle your school responsibilities better. We need better time-management ..."

Maeve lifted her tear-stained face. "You never hear the good stuff. Only the bad," she whispered.

Her mother stared at her. "What do you mean? Of course I hear the good stuff. But Maeve, this is serious. A 'zero'—this is an important signal ..."

A signal, Maeve thought bitterly. Like some sort of alien somewhere was trying to wave a flag and tell the whole universe: Maeve Kaplan-Taylor is a failure! She might look like she's doing OK in some things, but no! She's really a total failure.

She slumped down in the kitchen chair wishing she was somewhere else. All of the good stuff that had happened vanished, like bubbles that someone had poked with a pin. So what if she had come up with the blanket project? She was the only kid in the class who failed the math test.

"Carol," her father said gently. "I really think this is enough for now." He turned to Maeve. "Can we hear about something else? How are those blankets of yours coming along?"

"This is hardly the time," her mother interrupted.

But Maeve's father stood his ground. "I'd like to take you

and your friends over this week to drop them off," he said, handing Maeve a tissue. "What do you say about Friday? You guys all free?"

Maeve could barely speak over the lump in her throat. "Yes," she whispered. "I think so."

Her dad made her feel a tiny bit better. He leaned across the table and patted her hand. "We'll figure the math stuff out," he whispered. "And meanwhile, don't think it's the end of the world. Lots of smart people struggle with math ... maybe a new tutor will help."

Maeve's mother cleared her throat ominously. She didn't say anything, but she had that look on her face again. Mrs. Teague, Maeve's current tutor, had been her choice.

Maeve knew that her mom and dad would be up late again arguing. Over her. Once again, it was all her fault.

ଔ

Dear Maeve,

I feel sometimes like all I do is mess up. My mom wants me to be good at stuff that I'm not. And she doesn't seem to notice the things that I do well. The worst part is that my dad will sometimes take my side, and then my mom gets even madder.

— Confused

Maeve bit the top of her pen. Tonight, the words just seemed to come out of nowhere. She liked being "Ask Maeve." "Ask Maeve" always seemed to have the answers.

Dear Confused:

Remember, you don't have to be good at everything. Your mom already finished school. She had her chance to do things her way. Now you need to learn things your way. As for your parents ... well, it may not be up to you. Parents sometimes argue about their kids. But it isn't your fault.

Maeve buried her head in her oversized stuffed chicken, the way she used to when she was little. It sounded so sensible when she wrote it down. The question was, why didn't it feel like that in real life?

CHAPTER 21

❦

JERI'S PLACE

Charlotte's Journal
Thursday—late

No more mysterious notes from my secret friend. I wonder why not?

But I did get to the bottom of how my essay ended up in The Sentinel. Isabel confessed. She said it was almost an accident—I guess the paper slipped out of my notebook when I was trying to put it away. And she said almost before she knew it, she had turned it in on my behalf. I was upset at first, but she'd obviously meant well. Isabel really has a heart of gold, even if she can be impulsive at times. And anyway, I'm happy with the way things turned out. Isabel was right. I did want to try out for the paper, and somehow she must've sensed that.

Things have been better this week. Dad and I cooked together last night. His favorite "chili for wimps" recipe, which we haven't made in ages, and which doesn't burn your tongue off. It was fun, just the two of us, listening to

❀

music together and talking about the day. I love father-daughter cooking. I told dad I want to print up some of our favorite recipes in a book one day, and he thought that was a great idea. He said we should call it, "Cookin' and Chattin.'" That sounded good to me. I told him about The Sentinel, too—not about my piece coming out tomorrow, just about being on the staff, and how much fun it is. I even told him that Jennifer said I could be a "foreign correspondent" if we move to England. He just said "unh-hunh" with a distracted look on his face.

Tomorrow my piece comes out. I wonder if people will like it? I'm pretty nervous about peoples' reactions. You just never know. But as Avery always says, it's good to get stuff "out there."

The other big thing is that tomorrow afternoon we're taking the blankets to Jeri's Place. Maeve's dad is going to meet us after school and drive us down to Jamaica Plain, where the shelter is. I'm proud of Maeve. She's worked hard on this blanket project, and it really is a—what is the word she used to describe it to us once?—a "mitzvah." A good thing.

Well, I better take Marty out. He's doing his little "get me outside fast" dance. I'll write more tomorrow.

Maeve:
Notes to Self

1. Confirm time for Jeri's Place—find out where Dad can park the van.
2. Set up time for tutoring with Matt. He is so nice. I'm really glad dad found

him. I think it'll go much better if I work with him than with Mrs. Teague. My new deal is that I'll get lots of extra help with math if mom will let me keep working on the blankets during study hall.

3. Make a special mini-blanket for each of the girls. For Avery, one that says her favorite new saying: "Check all that apply." For Isabel, one with her cartoon character on it. For Charlotte, one with a constellation—what's that one she loves so much? Orion? And for Katani ... where would I be without Katani ... one that says something that I really want to tell her. "For Katani—who knows how to turn dreams into something that can really keep you warm."

Katani
Today's Horoscope

Virgo: *You are one of the most misunderstood of all the star signs. People think you're fussy and bad-tempered, but really you just like perfection. Virgos are highly intelligent and excellent workers. They like to use their heads. They have a tendency to express themselves through actions more than words.*

Today, avoid gossip and name-dropping. Your stars suggest that a new romance might be on the horizon. Friendships are very important this month. Something

that you have worked on very hard is about to bear fruit.
Lucky numbers: 42, 16. Avoid long-distance travel.

Avery's Blog
Online Journal:

```
   Not much new today at school. Here's a
question: Which is more statistically
likely, that I'll get hit by lightning
before eighth grade or that something
interesting will happen in math class?
   Random joke of the day:
   There's good news and bad news. The good
news is: you picked the winning number for
the Massachusetts lottery!
   The bad news is, you bought a New
Hampshire lottery ticket.
```

Ms. Rodriguez had a hard time getting everyone's attention in homeroom on Friday morning. The new edition of *The Sentinel* was out, and everyone was buried in the paper, hurrying to read what his or her classmates had written.

Charlotte really liked the way their stories looked in print. The front page, with school news, was entirely written by eighth and ninth graders. But on page 2, "Features," and page 3, "Arts," there were a bunch of stories by seventh graders. And the back page, devoted to Sports, had contributions from Dillon, Pete Wexler, and Avery.

Avery also had a short piece on the Features page, "Check All that Apply," asking interested students to email her with their thoughts about checking off boxes on standardized tests that identified you by race. Across the page from Avery's

BE PREPARED

You never know when you might have to stick your head in the sand!

EMERGENCY SAND

Isabel M.

piece was the "Ask Maeve" column. Charlotte's piece on community and belonging was set squarely in the upper middle of page 2.

"Nice," Avery said admiringly. "Prime real estate for your piece, Charlotte!"

Ms. Rodriguez could tell she wasn't going to have much luck getting them to put their newspapers away. Instead, she decided to make the paper the subject of their discussion. "Why don't we talk about the paper, and tell me what you've learned from this whole experience," she suggested.

Everyone was quiet for a minute. Maeve's hand shot up. "I've learned that giving advice is harder than you'd think," she said. Everyone laughed, but Maeve wasn't through. "I mean it," she said. "Coming up with problems ... that's kind of the easy part. But figuring out the solutions ... That's not so easy."

"You're right, Maeve. That sounds like a good lesson to take away from this," Ms. Rodriguez agreed.

Betsy's hand was up. "I learned that it's harder than I thought trying to get something done for a deadline," she said ruefully.

Anna whispered something to Joline, and Charlotte hid a smile. Leave it to the Queens of Mean to have managed not to learn much!

Charlotte raised her hand. "I learned that ..." She hesitated, glancing at Isabel. "That sometimes a little help can change your whole view of things," she said at last.

The comments came thick and fast then. Riley said he learned that he actually liked writing when it was something you cared about—namely, music. Pete said it was hard trying to be fair when you were covering a game. Avery said she learned that almost every reporter covering sports was a guy.

"These are all good lessons," Ms. Rodriguez commented. "And can I say something that I've learned from all of you? That working as a group, you were able to make an effective change in a longstanding school policy. You did some excellent writing. You challenged yourselves in new ways and opened the door for seventh graders to participate in the larger school community. You should all be very proud!"

"Hey," Nick said to Charlotte as they left homeroom ten minutes later. "I like what you wrote, Charlotte."

"You do?"

"Uh ..." Nick shifted his books a little, looking awkward. "I was wondering if you felt like doing something on Sunday. I was going to try to go hiking in the Blue Hills in the afternoon."

"That sounds like fun," Charlotte said. She didn't let herself even start to wonder whether it made sense to go, given her dad, and England, and the move. It was supposed to be warm again this weekend, Nick was nice—and Charlotte loved hiking. "Why not?" she said.

She didn't know why she was feeling so much better about everything, but she was. And even if she and her father were moving, there was no reason she couldn't get to know Nick better.

ᘓ

Maeve's father was waiting for them in the parking lot after school. "We have helpers!" Maeve cried joyfully, pointing to Nick, Dillon, Pete, and Riley who just happened to appear as Maeve was looking for helpers to move the cartons of blankets from room 206 to the back of her father's van.

"Good! Let's go," her father said cheerfully.

Even with the extra manpower, it took only two trips to get all of the blankets into the car. Maeve made sure that Dillon was on the other end of the carton she was carrying, which gave her ample time to flirt as they moved carefully down the hallway. Admittedly, trying to flirt and balance a big carton full of blankets at the same time wasn't the easiest. Finally Maeve just concentrated on not tripping.

"Phew. You guys have a lot of blankets here," Dillon said, after they'd managed to heave the last box into the back of the van.

"I know! I can't wait to deliver them." Maeve hopped up and down with excitement. "Jeri—she's the woman who runs Jeri's Place—says that they're waiting for us! We even get to meet some of the kids!"

✿

✿

"OK, crew. We should get going," her father said when the last carton was wedged into the van.

The ride to Jamaica Plain took about fifteen minutes.

"It's funny," Maeve said, when they found a parking place in front of the small gray building at 76 Parker Street. "I guess I kind of expected it to look ... I don't know. Poorer." She blushed a little. "Is that a totally ignorant thing to say?"

"Not everyone in a homeless shelter fits the stereotyped image," her father said mildly. "Sometimes people fall on hard times and just need a boost. Jeri's Place is famous for helping women and children—and they're often the ones who end up in bad circumstances if the mother loses her job or if her husband leaves ..."

"Yeah," Katani said. "There's a girl at my church who lived in a shelter for a few months when she was younger. Her dad moved out on them, and her mom couldn't keep up with the rent. The shelter helped her out while she found a new job."

Before they started unloading the back of the van, a young woman came out to greet them. Maeve was surprised again. She had expected Jeri to be much older.

It turned out that this was Jeri's daughter. "My name is Lorelei," she said, smiling. "So which one of you is the mastermind behind this great blanket idea?"

Maeve blushed deeply. She wouldn't have said anything, but Katani propelled her forward. "It's Maeve," Katani said.

"It's actually all of us," Maeve amended. They introduced themselves one by one.

"Well, I want to tell you, we are so excited and pleased about this project," Lorelei continued. "A lot of our clients are actually out working day-jobs now, but we thought you might want to bring your blankets right into our daycare center and drop them off yourselves. Are you up for that?"

Everyone nodded eagerly as Lorelei continued to explain. "Right now, we have about twenty children in our daycare program. They range from six weeks old to five years. Some of them have just joined us, but most have been here for at least a few months. Why don't you come on back, and introduce yourselves?"

Once again, Maeve found her expectations about the shelter changed once they stepped inside. It was a simple space but sparkling clean, with bright white walls. The dormitory space was upstairs. There was a comfortable lounge downstairs, and the daycare center looked ... well, more or less like the nursery school Maeve had gone to in the basement of the temple on Beacon Street. There was a blackboard on one wall, a whiteboard on another, boxes of plastic toys and puzzles, and a few beanbag chairs scattered around on a bright blue carpet. The kids were busy playing and reading, and a low hum of activity filled the room.

Lorelei said something to the woman who was sitting on the floor reading with several of the kids. "Children! Come on over! We have some exciting guests," the woman said, after introducing herself as Suzanne to the girls.

"It's the blanket girls!" one little girl cried, jumping up and down. "They told us you might come today!"

The next half-hour felt to Maeve like it was her birthday ... only better. She and the other girls sat on the floor next to the two cartons marked "toddlers" and "big kids," and each of the children came forward to choose a blanket. One little girl, Keisha, wrapped herself up in a soft lavender blanket decorated with a pink heart and started sucking her thumb. A boy named Marco helped himself to one of Avery's Red Sox blankets. The bigger kids helped the littlest kids to choose.

✿

And just as they'd finished making sure every child had a blanket, the doors opened and some of the older children started coming in from school. Some of the older boys just sat back and watched, but the older girls loved the blankets. Before they left the shelter, Keisha came running up, still clutching her lavender blanket. She pulled her thumb out and gave Maeve a hug.

"Thank you, blanket girl," she said.

Maeve hugged her back, her face warm with pleasure. This, she thought, was like getting an A+. A huge A+ that could never go away. She suddenly remembered something her mom said to her, "if you want to shine, you have to keep trying and never give up." Today all the Beacon Street Girls were shining.

Lorelei saw them out to the van afterwards. "Well, you sure brightened their day today," she said, shaking Maeve's hand one last time. "And I can tell you this—the women here are going to be every bit as happy for these blankets as Keisha was! Thanks, girls. And come visit us again—you don't need to bring us anything, but come and say hi!"

"We will!" everyone promised, as they piled back in to Maeve's dad's van. The funny thing was, Maeve knew that they weren't just saying it. She looked back at the shelter as they pulled away, and she had a definite feeling that they'd all be back.

CHAPTER 22

∞

THE ROOM IN THE PICTURE

"WHAT DO YOU guys think?" Katani asked, sitting back on her heels as she surveyed the Tower.

With Miss Pierce's help, they'd found a way to get Charlotte and her father out of the house for the day. She had invited them to go with her to the Observatory at Harvard, where a colleague of hers worked, and they were getting a special tour—which Miss Pierce promised would take several hours. After that, she was going to take them out for lunch. "They won't be back before 3:00," she promised Katani. "And I've left a key for you girls under the doormat. Good luck!"

Katani was the first to arrive. She had a carton of supplies with her—her glue gun, a bolt of material, her staple gun, paint ... the works. Isabel came next, with acrylic paints and a stretched canvas to make a sign. Then Avery, who'd brought a small end table as well as the blue lamp from her attic. Maeve was last. She'd brought cushiony material to cover the chair, and dozens of white stars that she'd cut out of construction paper. "I thought we could make that half of the room look like the night sky," she said. "Since Charlotte is so big on stars ... and that'll show that it's nighttime in the room."

"Great idea," Katani said. The girls set to work without a break. Once they really got started, there was more to do than they thought. Avery pulled the chair into one corner, and Maeve began to cover it. Isabel and Katani covered half of the room with navy blue fabric to look like the night sky, and Maeve hung up her stars on it.

"Hey, we should make that constellation she's always talking about," Maeve said. "Ryan or whatever."

"Orion, silly," Avery laughed. She paused. "Do you know what it looks like? I just remember that dog star—Sirius."

Maeve shrugged. "You know me. When I think 'stars,' it's Hollywood I'm seeing—not constellations."

"I've got to go downstairs anyway to Charlotte's apartment to get her copy of *Charlotte's Web*. I'll see if she has a star book, and I am going to take Marty out for a little run in the backyard." Avery said.

By 2 o'clock, the room was really beginning to shape up. The Lime Swivel chair had been completely transformed— covered with soft material, and then with the chintz fabric Katani had found, which seemed to exactly match the fabric in Charlotte's picture. The "night sky" looked wonderful— the navy fabric draped softly over the far windows, covered with stars—even with Orion, with his three bright stars forming a belt. The blue lamp glowed softly, and an open copy of *Charlotte's Web* lay face down on the cozy chair. Over the entrance, Isabel's whimsical sign hung with its bright lettering: "Welcome Home!"

"I think it's fantastic," Maeve said. "Come on guys. Let's print up the invitation, and get out of here!"

"Wait a minute," Katani said, studying the copy of Charlotte's photograph one last time. "Do you guys see something on the window in this picture?"

Everyone crowded around for a closer look.

"I think it's just a smudge on the lens cap," Avery said.

Maeve squinted. "Avery's right, Katani. It's nothing."

"No—it's a star!" Isabel gasped. "Let's put one of your stars on the window, Maeve!"

"Only we have to paint it blue. That star is blue—if it's a star," Avery said, still sounding skeptical.

One brush from Isabel's brush, and a blue star was ready to paste on the window.

"There!"

The girls looked around them, wonderingly. "It looks just like it," Maeve whispered. "It's the room in the picture!"

"Well, let's hope it works," Katani said briskly. "We don't want Charlotte to move. And we need something pretty powerful to keep her here at this point."

❧

"What a wonderful day," Mr. Ramsey said warmly to Miss Pierce, as they reached the front door of the house. "You were so great to take all the trouble to show us the Observatory. It was a real treat."

"Well, you'll have to come back when the Leonid Meteor showers fall," Miss Pierce said. She gave Charlotte a quick hug, glancing up almost despite herself at the trap door that led to the Tower.

I hope the girls managed to get everything done, she thought. It was 3:45, and the house was as quiet as if no one had come at all.

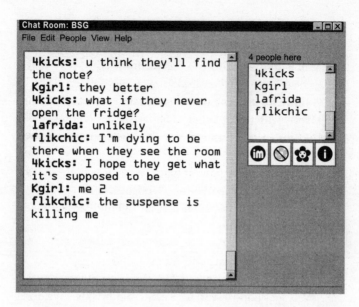

Chat Room: BSG
File Edit People View Help

4kicks: u think they'll find the note?
Kgirl: they better
4kicks: what if they never open the fridge?
lafrida: unlikely
flikchic: I'm dying to be there when they see the room
4kicks: I hope they get what it's supposed to be
Kgirl: me 2
flikchic: the suspense is killing me

4 people here

4kicks
Kgirl
lafrida
flikchic

"So what do you feel like for dinner?" Mr. Ramsey asked. It was 7 o'clock, already dark out, and the two of them were relaxing in the living room, trying to decide whether to go out and rent a video or to start an intensive Scrabble game instead.

"I'm kind of full from that huge lunch," Charlotte said. "What about you?"

"Maybe I'll go see what we've got. Could be a leftovers night," her father said, wandering into the kitchen.

Charlotte heard the fridge open, then silence.

"Charlotte, come here!" he called. "It looks like our mysterious letter writer has struck again!"

Charlotte hurried into the kitchen. Sure enough, the same cutout letters marched across the front of the envelope. "The Ramseys" it spelled out in many different-colored letters, all of different sizes.

"What does it say?" she demanded.

Mr. Ramsey opened up the letter. "Please go up to the Tower. A special message is waiting there for you." He cleared his throat. "From—your friends."

"Whoa," Charlotte said, taking a deep breath. "That's so weird!" She glanced up at the trap door to the Tower room, goose bumps rising on her arms. "I'm kind of scared," she whispered. "Do you think it's something creepy, like in one of those horror movies?"

"I don't think so," her father said, laughing. "But all the same, let's go see what's up there. I wouldn't mind getting to the bottom of these mystery letters." He opened the top drawer of one of the cupboards, pulling out a flashlight. "We might need this," he said.

Charlotte grabbed Marty. "I'm bringing him with us," she said, burrowing her face in his soft fur.

"Great. He can protect us," her father teased her. Tiny and cuddly as he was, Marty wasn't exactly a fierce watchdog!

"You go first," Charlotte said, holding back a little.

She followed her father up the steep staircase, her heart beating harder each time that a stair creaked. It felt like forever before they made it to the top of the stairs and her father flung open the trapdoor, climbing up into the Tower. Charlotte was right behind him.

"Welcome Home," she read softly, puzzling over the painted letters.

Her father opened the door and they stepped inside.

For a minute, Charlotte's eyes had to get used to the change in light. A lamp was glowing softly in one corner; otherwise the room was almost dark. She could see white stars flickering on a dark background that looked like the night sky.

"Daddy, it's Orion!" she cried in excitement, racing over

to touch the constellation.

Her father was staring with a dazed look at the corner.

"I don't understand," he faltered. "Who could have done this? Who knew ...?"

Charlotte turned and followed his gaze. For a minute she didn't say a word. Then a cry escaped from her, almost unconsciously. It was the room in her picture! The blue lamp, the flowered chair ...

"Even my book," she whispered. "It's just like in the picture."

"What picture?" her father asked her. Then, as if in a trance, he walked over to the chair.

"Even your sticker is here," he murmured. "It's your bedroom from when you were a little girl, Charlotte. At Arlington Street. Remember?"

Charlotte gazed around her in wonder. But how could this be, she thought. Unless ...

Suddenly, she remembered Isabel asking her if she could borrow her picture. They must have sneaked in here and transformed the Tower room, she thought. They found my favorite picture, and they wanted to make the Tower room look like home!

She was about to tell her father what must have happened when she realized that he was crying. He sat right down on the floor of the Tower room, wiping his eyes. The next thing she knew, he had taken her in his arms and was hugging her tightly, as if he never wanted to let her go.

"Charlotte," Mr. Ramsey said brokenly, "I miss her so much! I tried to tell myself that it would be OK—that I could manage. But I don't think I ever let myself really grieve for her the way that I needed to. All those years—in Africa, and Australia, and Europe—I felt like the farther away that I went, the easier it would be to start life over."

He paused, wiping his eyes again. "And then I thought that it might help to come back here. To start over here, where we were all together as a family. And it's been so hard!"

"Oh, Daddy." Charlotte hugged him. "It's OK. If you hate being back here, we can move again. I'll be fine, I promise!"

Mr. Ramsey shook his head, looking in wonder around the room. "No, Charlotte. That's not the answer. Your friends—I'm guessing that they're the ones who made this room look like this—they're really right. This is home, where we are right now—today. Moving to England isn't going to solve any of my problems. Charlotte, I need to start building my life again—without your mother. Painful as it is, I can't get her back—however far and wide I search for her."

Charlotte stared at him. "You mean it, Dad? You really want to stay?"

He nodded. "I do, Charlotte. We have good friends here. I like my job a lot, and even if it may not be the 'job of a lifetime,' it's interesting and fun, and it's keeping me busy. I love our new home. I love seeing you settled." He looked around him, clearing his throat. "I think I started to realize this last Saturday, when you and I went back to all the places we used to go to when you were little. I want to stay here and build a life together again—the two of us."

Charlotte flung her arms around him. "I'm so happy," she cried.

She could hardly believe it. The Tower room and Marty and Miss Pierce and Ms. Rodriguez and Social Dancing and Nick and the bakery and Irving's Toy and Card Shop and most of all, her beloved friends—she wouldn't have to leave them after all!

"But Dad," she asked, lifting her head and studying him

closely, "you're sure you're not giving up on your dream?"

"Charlotte, my dream right now is to make a great home for us," her father said slowly. "I think it's taken me a while to figure that out, but that's what I want most. Oxford's been around a long time—it won't disappear! For now, I think we should stay put. You think you can stand to settle down and stay in one place for a good long time? You don't think you'll go stir-crazy?"

"I think I'll manage," Charlotte assured him, jumping to her feet. "I think I'll manage just fine!"

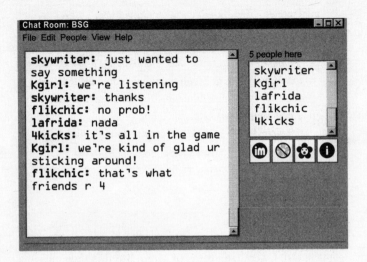

Chat Room: BSG

File Edit People View Help

skywriter: just wanted to
say something
Kgirl: we're listening
skywriter: thanks
flikchic: no prob!
lafrida: nada
4kicks: it's all in the game
Kgirl: we're kind of glad ur
sticking around!
flikchic: that's what
friends r 4

5 people here

skywriter
Kgirl
lafrida
flikchic
4kicks

Charlotte's Journal
Late Sunday night

So that's that. No moves planned for this family!

Marty looks happy. He's pretty snug here, right on
the end of my bed. Anyway, I found out that they don't
take dogs into England until they've been in quarantine
for six whole months. That's because they don't want any
rabies coming into the country. And Marty is not the kind
of dog who would tolerate quarantine.

I showed dad my piece in the school paper tonight
after I got back from hiking with Nick. He got all misty-
eyed and said he thinks that I could be a famous writer
one day. We'll have to see. I might decide to be an explorer
instead. Nick and I were talking on our hike today and we
both really love the idea of going to Patagonia ... or maybe
down to the South Pole, to see the penguins.

❀

When I told dad, he groaned. "I thought we just decided that we're staying put for a while!" he said.

I cracked up ... big time. It's true—there's a wonderful big world out there to explore, and one day I want to see as much of it as I possibly can. But for now, it's pretty great just being right here.

I reached over to tickle Marty's stomach and tried saying what Isabel wrote on her sign. It sounded pretty good, and I said it again, right into the soft velvety spot on the top of Marty's head.

Welcome home.

Guess what I just saw outside my window? The first star coming out. Of course I think of Mom. But this time, not in a sad way. She always said, *my wish is that your wish will come true.* And you know what?

This time, it really did.

℞

To be continued ...

THE NEW TOWER RULES
CREATED BY THE NEWEST ORDER
OF THE RUBY AND THE SAPPHIRE

Be it resolved that all girls are created equal!

1. We will speak our minds, but we won't be like obnoxious or anything.
2. We won't put ourselves down, even if we aren't super-smart, super-coordinated, or a supermodel.
3. We'll be loyal to our friends and won't lie to them even if they make a mistake or do something totally embarrassing.
4. We will go for it—how will we know what we can do if we don't try?
5. We will try to eat healthy and stay active. How can you chase your dream if you can't keep up?
6. We won't just take from people and the planet. We'll try to give back good things too.

ɞ .... ઝ

Amendments:

1. We can add as many amendments as we
   like.
2. We will dare to be fashion
   individualistas—like we're all
   different so why should we dress the
   same?
3. Sometimes we'll veg out—just because
   we feel like it!
4. We should try to save money so if we
   ever want to, we can start a business
   or something someday.
5. We should have as much fun as we can.

Note from Katani
Proposed new amendment:

6. We will try to keep an open mind about
   new people.

What's the vote?

Avery—sounds great!
Charlotte—this has my vote!
Maeve—I love new people!
Isabel—I'm happy!

Book Club Buzz

10 QUESTIONS FOR YOU AND YOUR FRIENDS TO CHAT ABOUT

1. Why is it complicated for a new girl to become friends with the Beacon Street Girls?

2. How do Charlotte, Katani, Avery, and Maeve each react to Isabel?

3. Why is Charlotte so sad about facing another move if she is used to being a Global Girl?

4. What do you think about the schemes that the Beacon Street Girls come up with to try to change Mr. Ramsey's mind?

5. What does the blanket project teach the girls about working together?

6. Why is it important to have grown-ups in your life—like Miss Pierce, Mrs. Fields, Ethel Weiss, and Ms. Rodriguez—to talk to besides your parents?

7. What do you like about Maeve's blanket project?

8. Have you ever coordinated a community service project? If so, what did you do to make it a success?

9. How does Charlotte eventually convince her father to stay in Brookline?

10. What does Charlotte teach her father about accepting the past?

1. What is Charlotte's cooking specialty?
   A. frog's legs
   B. chicken parmesan
   C. herbed scrambled eggs with grated French gruyère cheese
   D. goat cheese salad with apples and walnuts

2. What book is the Abigail Adams Jr. High seventh grade class reading? (Hint: Charlotte reads ahead because she loves it so much!)
   A. *To Kill a Mockingbird*
   B. *Charlotte's Web*
   C. *A Day No Pigs Would Die*
   D. *Treasure Island*

3. What state did Isabel live in before she came to Brookline?
   A. Michigan
   B. Mississippi
   C. Colorado
   D. California

4. Who does Charlotte first tell about her fears that she and her dad might be moving to England?
   A. Katani
   B. Miss Pierce
   C. Mrs. Fields
   D. Marty

5. What kind of creature does Isabel use in her first cartoon?
   A. penguin
   B. ostrich
   C. tiger
   D. bear

6. Who is G.H. in Anna and Joline's gossip column?
   A. George Huron
   B. Gina Heckle
   C. Gordie Hines
   D. Gianna Hillman

7. Katani's sign is:
   A. Taurus
   B. Aries
   C. Aquarius
   D. Virgo

8. Who is Maeve's partner at Social Dance class?
   A. Sammy Andropovitch
   B. Robert Worley
   C. Dillon Johnson
   D. Riley Lee

9. Which of these did the BSG not do to convince Mr. Ramsey to stay in Brookline?
   A. decorate the Tower just like Charlotte's old room on Arlington Street
   B. write to Oxford and say no to the job offer
   C. get Charlotte to use reverse psychology
   D. leave anonymous letters for Mr. Ramsey and Charlotte

10. Which BSG got "Feature Writer" on *The Sentinel*?
    A. Katani
    B. Charlotte
    C. Maeve
    D. Avery

(Answers right below!)

SCORING

8-10 Points: Congrats ... You're a Beacon Street Girl at heart! We can never have too many BFFs!

5-7 Points: Nice work ... How 'bout we hang out at Montoya's after school?

0-4 Points: No problem ... let's go get some Swedish Fish!

ANSWERS: 1. C. herbed scrambled eggs with grated French gruyère cheese **2. A.** *To Kill a Mockingbird* **3. A.** Michigan **4. D.** Marty **5. A.** penguin **6. C.** Gordie Hines **7. D.** Virgo **8. D.** Riley Lee **9. B.** write to Oxford and say no to the job offer **10. B.** Charlotte

sneak preview!

Chat Room: BSG

File Edit People View Help

flikchic: u guys are gonna luv me!
Kgirl: well we already do but y?
flikchic: dad is giving me tix to the red sox game!!
4kicks: ur dad is my hero!
lafrida: i love baseball
skywriter: me too!
4kicks: since ur in a giving mood, how 'bout lending me ur guinea pigs for a while?
skywriter: i think that's what they call pushing your luck
lafrida: lol
flikchic: no way, ave ... my little babies are escape artists—u can't handle them
4kicks: i can! i'm fast
flikchic: we'll see ... ooo, i 4got! dillon started to ask me something 2day, but he stopped and got all red ... think he likes me?
skywriter: could be!
lafrida: dillon's so nice
flikchic: btw, mom says the fam has to have a big talk
Kgirl: uh-oh
flikchic: i wonder what it's about?

5 people here

flikchic
Kgirl
4kicks
lafrida
skywriter

Have you seen

www.beaconstreetgirls.com ?

MEET THE BSG | EXPLORE THEIR WORLD | PLAY GAMES | DOWNLOAD STUFF | BOOKS ★★★ SHOP

new!
Make a friendship bracelet

 Welcome!

BSG Poll

Who do you feel most like today?

○ Maeve
○ Avery
○ Katani
○ Isabel
○ Charlotte

Take our poll and see what other BSG girls said.

done

August 28, 2006 **Top Picks**

SECRET TOWER
Find out more about the secret BSG meeting spot!

ISABEL'S RECIPES
You don't want to miss these scrumptious treats from Isabel's kitchen!

BSG JIGSAW JAM
We've got more puzzles! Help put the pieces together.

AVERY'S BLOG
This girl speaks her mind ... about dogs, sports, and what rules she'd like to change.

More **FUN!**

Games   Quizzes
Recipes   Shopping
Crafts   Contests

Which BSG are **you**?